MW01134142

ANNA MAY WONG

— HOLLYWOOD LEGEND —

William Wong Foey

ANNA MAY WONG
HOLLYWOOD LEGEND
Copyright © 2018 by William Wong Foey

All rights reserved. No portion of this book may be reproduced in
any form—mechanically, electronically, or by any other means,
including photocopying, recording, or by any information storage
and retrieval system—without permission in writing from the
author.

ISBN 978-1717428110

Printed in the United States of America
First Printing, 2018

Dedication

Dedicated to
Mama On
Marna Whitley
And to minorities and women everywhere who had to
battle for their identity and self-worth.

And to Goo Goo (1966-1976)

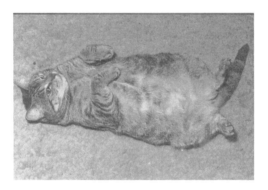

Author's Note

Anna May Wong was never intended to be a factual account of this remarkable actress's life. My intention was to pay homage to a woman who fought crushing racism for her own self-worth and dignity.

Even now, in the 21st century, Asian performers still struggle to fine their rightful place. To date, Ms. Wong is still the world's only true female Asian film star.

Any depiction of real-life characters in my novel was not intended to cast them in a negative light, but was meant solely for dramatic effect.

— William Wong Foey

Chinese Terminology

domo arigato: Japanese for "thank you"

gai jin: Japanese term for "foreigner," used in a derogatory manner.

gim sam: Chinese term for California/America, meaning "Gold Mountain"

Gold Mountain: Chinese term for California

gwah lo: derogatory term for white people, loosely translated as "old rice"

hak gwai: derogatory term for black people

nui doi: Chinese for "little girl"

xi e xie (pronounced "shay shay"): Chinese for "thank you" in the Mandarin dialect

1

"We will have a grand celebration for my strong, brave son. He is about to enter the world now!" exclaimed Wong Sam Sing as he watched his wife give birth.

With encouraging words from their midwife, Sue May, Sam Sing's wife, Lee You, fought through the terrible pain. Although she wanted to scream at the top of her lungs, she did not out of fear of showing weakness to her husband.

Gradually, the newborn's feet, then legs, came forward.

The father grinned with great joy. "I love you, my son," spoke Sam Sing under his breath. Abruptly, his joy erupted into deep anger. "The child has no manhood! It is a worthless nui doi! A girl!" voiced Sam Sing dejectedly.

"Sir, she is a very beautiful baby. You should be proud," interjected the midwife.

"She is my daughter—*our* daughter. Sue May is right, you should be proud. We will call her Li Tsong. Her gwah lo name will be Anna May Wong, according to the gwah lo's custom of the first name first and the last name last," added Lee You.

"In Mother China, daughters are worthless. Some families I knew back in my homeland even drowned girl babies," exclaimed Sam Sing.

"Husband, this is not China. Do you forget that we now reside in Gim Sam, the Gold Mountain — California? Only a monster would kill their own child, not to mention that such an act in the land of the gwah los is called murder, which is illegal."

"Damn the gwah los." Sam Sing fought back tears. "I was only five when I arrived on the Gold Mountain with my parents. I am now past forty, close to middle-age, and the gwah los still have never made me feel like I belong here. The gwah los would spit on me when I was a child. It is hard enough to be a chink man in the land of gwah los, let alone a chink female."

Lee You struggled to sit up. She gazed at baby Anna, strongly concerned for her daughter's future.

"My husband, this is 1905 by gwah lo years. The world is changing rapidly. The dowager herself is losing the firm grip she held on our mother country for so long. The peasants of China are demanding reform. It is no longer necessary for one to have something dangling between one's legs to carry their own weight in the world," strongly stated the protective mother. "Please allow me to hold my daughter," she added.

Sam Sing shook his head. "A changing world does not necessarily make a better world, my wife. Anna's grandmother had bound feet — the sign of beauty and upper-class status. She understood her place and did not complain."

Lee You was perspiring heavily, and fatigued after giving birth, but nonetheless managed to stand up with assistance from the midwife. She held Anna high toward the stars that shone brightly through the bedroom window. "Husband, your grandmother was taught to keep her thoughts to herself. What kind of foolish woman would enjoy having disfigured feet and a lifetime of pain, shuffling about, never able to walk normally? Anna will be her own woman," proclaimed Lee You.

Sam Sing stormed out of the room without further comment. He walked downstairs to the laundry shop he owned and pulled out a bottle of fine whiskey which he kept locked in his desk. He placed an empty glass on the desk, ready to pour himself a drink. As he was about to pour the whiskey, he stopped after seeing his reflection in the storefront window. Sam picked up the glass and threw it violently against the wall. It shattered into a million pieces. He took a long swallow of the strong liquor straight from the bottle.

"I am a man! Why do I not feel like one? Goddamn gwah los — or should I say white people — made me think I am not one," reflected Sam Sing.

He proceeded to get very drunk throughout the rest of the night.

2

Time began to pass slowly for the Wong family. The invisible wall Sam Sing constructed between him and his daughter Anna seemed to grow thicker and higher each day.

The troubled man buried his soul and every fiber of his being in work and strong liquor. He alienated himself from his wife as well, and Lee You felt as worthless and unwanted as her daughter. While her husband found solace in the bottle, she escaped the pain and sorrow by becoming a workaholic.

In her first few years of life, Anna's only companion, and the only person who gave her any attention, was the midwife Sue May. She used her own money to take the precious girl to the new entertainment invention, the Nickelodeon.

Even before Anna was old enough to attend kindergarten, she watched in awe the shadowy, flickering images that flashed across the silver screen. She understood almost entirely the words spoken and the nature of the larger-than-life melodramas. In her formative years, she and her nursemaid were forced to sit in the seats on the far side of the theater — never in the center seats, which were reserved for the gwah los.

Such was Anna's introduction to racism. It certainly would not be her last. But it was at that early age that she felt her calling to become an actress.

Once, at the age of five, she sneaked into her mother's bedroom. Like any inquisitive child, Anna rummaged through her mother's closet and drawers. She played dress-up and adorned herself in an exquisite yellow silk dress patterned with lotus blossoms. She smeared lipstick across her tiny mouth and wrapped red ribbons tightly around her bare feet. Shuffling with the long dress dragging behind her, she stood before her mother's full-length mirror.

Anna mouthed words without speaking to imitate the beautiful gwah lo femme fatales she was mesmerized by in the silent movies.

"What the hell are you doing, daughter!" screeched Lee You as she entered the bedroom.

Anna stood frozen, afraid to speak.

Lee You had just returned from smoking opium for several hours in the basement, where she would not be disturbed. She reeked of the sickly sweet smell of the narcotic smoke. Her eyes were glazed over, her stance unsteady.

"Little brat! How dare you wear my favorite formal dress! You smear your face with red lipstick — you resemble a gwah lo tramp!" screamed Lee You in hysterical anger.

The mother violently tore the dress off little Anna and repeatedly struck her face. Then, feeling this was not a severe enough punishment, she grabbed a wooden coat hanger and beat Anna savagely across her buttocks. "How dare you wrap your feet in ribbons! You pretend to be Mama See, who had bound feet? You think it is a sign of upper class? More like an upper-class slave. Like your grandmother, I am only an unpaid servant and babysitter," exclaimed Lee You. She continued to beat Anna until she bled.

As she raised her arm for another blow, a firm hand gripped her mother's wrist. It was the hand of the nursemaid, Sue May.

"Mrs. Wong! You shame your daughter and you shame yourself. Where is that sharp-tongued woman who spoke up for her daughter's rights on the day she was born? Who are you punishing? Your daughter or yourself?"

Tears streamed down Lee You's face as she gazed down at the small, naked girl, who was shaking and covered with blood.

Unlike most small children who are physically abused, Anna did not scream or cry, but rather stared at her mother curiously, as if to ask...why?

"Oh Lord Buddha, what have I done! I am a lost Chinese woman." She asked Sue May to fetch her a robe, bandages, and medication.

After dressing Anna's wounds, Lee You placed a soft cotton robe over her battered body. Then she cradled Anna in her arms, softly rocking her back and forth.

"My apologies, Anna. You are my only daughter. You are so very precious to me. I suppose I was jealous. You will someday have the freedom and good life I wanted so much for myself, but never had."

Mature beyond her years, Anna reached her right hand up to her mother's face and touched her lips lovingly. "Mama, someday I will be a great actress and we will be happy forever."

In that moment, mother and daughter felt a bond, if only temporary, while her father remained cold and distant, wallowing in his own self-pity.

Lee You placed Anna in her bed, which she had not shared with Sam Sing since Anna's birth. She instructed Sue May to sit with her daughter while she left to have a word with her husband.

Upon entering Sam's bedroom without knocking, she was not surprised to see her husband sharing his bed with a much younger woman.

"Shin-oh, you are paid to launder clothes, not satisfy my husband's hearty appetite for young ladies!" Savagely, Lee You yanked the nude girl out of Sam's bed. "Get out!" she screamed while throwing the girl her clothes. "Whore!" Lee You shouted. She slammed the door, which hit the young girl's buttocks as she rushed out of the bedroom.

Once the mistress girl was gone, Lee You stood towering over Sam Sing as he drank from a whiskey bottle he had sitting on the nightstand.

"My husband, we must stop the misery we are causing our daughter."

She snatched the bottle from his hand and flung it out the open window.

"Damn it, wife, that was a twelve-year-old, single-barrel whiskey."

"Sit up," commanded Lee You. Doing as he was told, Sam Sing sat up and rested his back and head against the headboard.

Lee You sat on the bed beside Sam. "Husband, the devil has a strong grip on our souls."

Sam Sing grinned oddly. He took a pack of cigarettes and matches off the nightstand and offered a cigarette to his wife. "Wife, let me tell you a story I never told anyone. Something quite ugly happened to my father and his first wife, who was pregnant with their first child. One day, she became very ill. My father sent for the gwah lo doctor to come to her aid, but he refused to help. The white doctor explained to him that he did not treat chinks. My father's first wife and unborn child died the next morning. The unborn baby was a boy, and the mother was only nineteen. I am the product of my father's second wife."

Lee You rudely blew cigarette smoke into Sam Sing's face. "And your point is?" she asked.

Sam Sing shrugged his shoulders. "I do not know if there is a point, other than on the Gold Mountain the gwah los are God and both a Chinese man and woman should know their place. Our disrespectful little girl, Anna, is constantly ranting about being a moving-picture actress. In our homeland, only whores are actresses and only male actors are respected."

"My husband, why is it you never told me of this bit of sadness in your family's past before?"

Sam Sing chuckled softly. "In ancient China they would torture a man with a 'thousand cuts' before the poor man finally died. What happened to my father and his first wife was only one of many insulting cuts the gwah los have inflicted on my yellow people, on black people, brown, whatever. I thought to not speak of such obscenities would help me forget —but obviously not."

Lee You rose off the bed. "Husband, we have all suffered. You drown out all the wrongs against you with the bottle, while I drown my misfortunes with tar opium and hard work. We have forgotten that we have a daughter who needs to be understood and encouraged, or we will be damned," she voiced. She stormed away.

Sam Sing continued to drink whiskey after Lee You departed, reflecting on his wife's criticism of the both of them.

"Lee You, I salute you for being the man I am not," spoke Sam Sing to himself.

3

At age five, Anna, by law, was required to begin attending grade school. Lee You and Sue May escorted Anna to the public school kindergarten. After entering the classroom an hour late on the first day of school, Anna refused to release her grip on her mother's and nursemaid's hands.

"Mrs. Wong your daughter is late for the first day of school," said the matronly looking Mrs. Whitworth.

"My deepest apologies, Mrs. Whitworth. Anna can be stubborn, but she is a good girl." Lee You turned to her daughter. "Anna, you mind and do what Mrs. Whitworth asks of you," she ordered, having to pry Anna's hands off her skirt as she and Sue May attempted to leave.

Mrs. Whitworth firmly took hold of Anna's shoulders, pushing her forcefully to a desk that had a tiny child's chair.

Defiantly, Anna stood up and attempted to run away. Mrs. Whitworth slapped her hand with a wooden ruler. Although the ruler stung Anna's hand, she did not display any pain, but rather kicked the elderly woman in the shins. The teacher cried out and bit her tongue to prevent herself from cursing in front of the children.

The classroom, filled with children Anna's age, burst out in laughter.

"Silence, you naughty brats!" commanded the teacher. Deeply angered, Mrs. Whitworth grabbed Anna by her shiny black hair and towed her back to the chair. "I should have known. You Celestials are nothing but trouble. You wicked little girl! You and your people should have stayed in China where you belong. But, Miss Wong,

9

since I am stuck with you, you *will* behave. If you want a test of wills, you will lose," stated the stern instructor.

Such was Anna's introduction to public school on the Gold Mountain. Throughout her grammar school education, Anna tolerated taunts and abuse from her follow gwah lo classmates, and even a number of her teachers, who would treat her with racist undertones.

On one particularly bad day, while in sixth grade, a clique of white students cruelly tied Anna to a tree with a jump rope, then taunted her with racist remarks and spit on her. Her inner strength prevented Anna from giving them the satisfaction of seeing her cry or begging to be released.

One of the mean-spirited boys attempted to kiss the restrained Anna. "Hey, chink girl, why you fighting me? I bet you've never been kissed by a handsome white boy. You should enjoy it."

As the attacker licked Anna's face, a strong hand spun the bully abruptly around. A big, ham-like fist knocked the offender to the ground. Towering over the prostrate lad stood a boy of the same age.

"Marion, you had no right to hit me. Me and my buddies were just fun'n. We didn't mean any harm," spoke the bully as his friends helped him to his feet.

"Bastards," cried Anna's rescuer as he knocked the bully down a second time. "Joe, I was just fun'n too. Now, you assholes go pick on someone else," shouted Anna's savior.

Pulling their friend up once again, the boys swiftly stepped away. "Chink lover!" shouted the boys as they ran off.

"Missy, they had you a bit outnumbered," quipped the twelve-year-old boy, who was quite tall and husky for his age. "My name's Marion Morrison," he said as he untied Anna.

"Thank you, Marion. My name is Anna May Wong."

"Right pretty name. Call me Duke. My kid brother named me after the family dog."

Anna was quite taken with the tall, blue-eyed gwah lo boy. "Marion…uh, Duke...you are very kind. I was born on the Gold

Mountain but I do not feel American."

Duke smoothed out Anna's ruffled hair. "Gold Mountain? You mean the name your people have for California? Hell, I'm a stranger here too. My family and I just immigrated to the Gold Mountain from Iowa — or as us backwoods boys there would say, 'I-uh-way,'" spoke Duke with a big grin.

Anna hugged the kind boy. She felt a strange feeling of attraction and bewilderment, this being the first time she had ever closely touched a gwah lo — and a boy, at that.

"*Xie xie,* my hero," said Anna, thanking the boy in her Chinese language.

Over the next few years, Duke and Anna became good friends, with Duke always coming to her rescue when faced with school bullies. She began to have a schoolgirl crush — but being tall and handsome, Duke had countless female admirers. It broke Anna's heart when the always candid young man informed her that he felt nothing but warm friendship for her. Deeply saddened, Anna's desire to act and appear in the fledgling industry called "motion pictures" became more obsessive than ever before, to help her deal with the feelings she had for the lanky boy with the dazzling eyes. She reminded herself that her parents would never approve of any romantic relationship with a gwah lo, and therefore, a relationship with Duke would not have worked out in any case.

At fourteen, Anna no longer had the need for a nanny. She began stealing pennies from the laundry till and making excuses that she had to go to the public library for her school studies. Then she would rush to see whatever recent "flickers" were showing at the Nickelodeon, often skipping school to attend matinees. Sitting alone in the darkness, she would mouth the words, displayed at the bottom of the screen in subtitles, of the primary female characters.

One late afternoon, Anna walked out of the theater entranced after watching the silent screen movie star Lillian Gish in one of her signature films, *Way Down East.*

What a brave gwah lo woman to float so dangerously on a chunk of ice, and be rescued by a cute gwah lo man just before she was about to plunge over a high waterfall, Anna thought.

She climbed the stairs to her family's residence above the laundry and gradually opened the door, hoping no one would notice her entrance. But to her chagrin, there stood her parents, waiting impatiently for their delinquent daughter.

"Daughter, where have you been?" asked Sam Sing.

"You must have a photographic memory to study at the library, taking no schoolbooks, paper, pens or pencils with you," interjected Lee You.

Anna grinned nervously. "Oh, yes, Papa, Mama. I mostly go to the library to read books," replied Anna sheepishly.

Her father shouted, "Daughter, you make a poor liar. Your teacher paid us a visit shortly after you left for the 'library' — ha! She informed us that you did not attend school the last two days and you also missed a couple of days last week. In fact, you only attend school half the time. The teacher thought we were forcing you to work in the laundry rather than allow you to attend school full-time. She warned your mother and me about the child labor laws on the Gold Mountain."

Lee You grabbed Anna's shoulders and shook her fiercely. "Daughter, I have argued with your father many times that you were special and you needed space to find yourself, but not at the expense of getting a proper education. Furthermore, I have heard from your Chinese classmates that you have been seeing a gwah lo boy! Daughter, you need to stay within your race! A gwah lo boyfriend will only break your heart."

Sam Sing barked, "Anna, you shame your parents and you shame your Chinese heritage! From now on we will address you by your Chinese name, Liu Tsong."

"Mother, Father," Anna protested, "I have no boyfriend, gwah lo or otherwise. I want to be an actress. It is in my blood. Please, I beg you, my parents, set me free."

"This is the Gold Mountain," her father replied. "Only the gwah los are free. Your foolish mother believes that because we now live in the twentieth century, the world will change. Perhaps so, but the gwah los do not change. I am good enough to clean their shirts and soiled undergarments, but the white devils will never invite your mother and me to their homes for coffee and cake. Know your place, my daughter. Know your place," advised Sam Sing.

Lee You wrapped her arms around Anna, kissing her on the forehead. "Anna...uh, Liu Tsong, come. It is time for dinner. I've prepared your favorite war wonton soup with fresh abalone."

Anna pushed her mother away. "Father, Mother, I know my place and it is not to spend my life above a laundry sleeping alone, then dying alone. Someday I will be very special. I'll show you!" exclaimed Anna. She turned and ran out the door.

"Liu Tsong! Anna! Please stop!" shouted Lee

"You attempting to chase after her?" Sam Sing grabbed her wrists, holding her back. "Let the little brat go. She has never obeyed me. When she grows hungry and cold, you will see your daughter soon enough, my wife."

Anna wandered about the streets of Los Angeles — a far different community in 1919 than the megalopolis it would soon become. She reflected on how empty and meaningless her young life had been. She always felt terribly alone, though she had befriended Duke. But she was only one of many friends the charming boy had, and even what little casual relationship she had with Duke would fade after a few years. Anna did not make friends easily, even with Chinese youth her own age.

"Where do I belong?" whispered Anna, her feet becoming blistered after walking for hours.

She dreamed of being a movie actress in an industry that was only a little older than she was. But despite her youth, she understood that in all the flickers she had watched and memorized, there only appeared gwah lo actors and actresses. It would be an uphill battle for anyone to obtain movie stardom, let alone an inexperienced Chinese girl without connections.

The day had now turned to full darkness. Despite being very cold and hungry, Anna's stubborn pride prevented her from returning home. Even had she been inclined to do so, she was lost and her blistered, swollen feet would prevent her from making the journey.

She removed her shoes and lay face up in the middle of the street. "I wanted so much. I was going to move heaven and earth to become a moving-picture actress, but if I cannot have this, let me die quickly. With a little luck, a swift car will run over my head and end my agony," voiced Anna weakly.

The cold, hard pavement hurt her back as she gazed up at the brilliant stars. She longed to be among them.

4

Moving in and out of a fitful slumber, Anna slept in the middle of the street. A long, sleek car approached. The driver saw the motionless girl lying in the roadway. Slamming on the brakes, the tires locked up and billowed out a foul blue smoke as the Rolls Royce screamed to a halt. The left front tire stopped only a scant few inches from Anna's head.

An alarmed chauffeur, dressed in an all-black cap and uniform, rushed to Anna's aid. A sharply dressed, redheaded woman standing barely five feet tall followed quickly behind him.

"Hector, did you kill this Asian girl with my Rolls?" asked the woman.

"Miss Gish, I beg you, I never touched the young lady. I did not strike her with the Rolls, madam. She was already lying on the street before the car came anywhere near her. The Rolls never touched a hair on her head."

Miss Gish raised Anna's head and gently rubbed her cheek. "What a dear young girl she is. Hector, place her in the car. We must determine the seriousness of her injuries and the mystery of why she is lying in the middle of a city street at this hour."

"Yes, madam," replied the chauffeur as he carefully carried Anna to the back seat of the Rolls Royce.

Anna's eyes opened. As they came into focus, she saw an angelic face grinning warmly at her.

"Ah, young lady, I am so pleased to see you are awake. Are you injured? Ill?"

Frightened and confused, Anna surveyed her surroundings. It

15

appeared she was lying in a brass, four-poster bed in a bedroom adorned with expensive paintings.

"I—I am not sick. I am not hurt. Only very tired," replied Anna.

The woman placed a moist face towel on Anna's forehead. "How delightful. From the appearance of the soles of your feet, you have journeyed a long way. You need rest and nourishment. Please allow me to introduce myself. I am Lillian Gish. And your name, young lady?"

"Anna May Wong," she responded reluctantly.

Lillian shook Anna's hand. "Excellent, very pleased to meet such a lovely young lady. You are Chinese, I presume?"

Anna nodded her head.

"Miss Wong — uh, may I address you as Anna?"

Anna nodded.

"Splendid! Anna, right now you must eat, then rest, my child. We will have plenty of time to get acquainted later."

Lillian kissed Anna's hand, then rang a bell. A few minutes later, a maid entered the room.

"Mindy, bring Miss Wong a sandwich and some milk," ordered Gish.

Ravenous, Anna practically inhaled the food. When she was finished, she nestled into the luxurious bed. The silk sheets embraced her like a baby in the womb. It had been a long, hard day, and although she was lying in a strange bed in a stranger's home, Anna felt secure and content. She had seen the petit redheaded gwah lo woman before, but she could not remember when or where.

After a long, restful sleep, Anna was awakened by a soft knock on the door.

"Good morning, Miss Wong," said the maid. "Here are some fresh clothes for you to wear. These belonged to Miss Gish. Being a small lady, her clothes should fit you well. After you have freshened up and dressed, Miss Gish would like you to join her. I will wait for you." The maid closed the bedroom door and waited in the hallway.

After washing and dressing in the pretty blue dress she had been given, Anna was escorted down the wide mahogany staircase. They entered a grand dining hall with crystal chandeliers.

An elderly man dressed in a butler's suit pulled out Anna's chair. She stood, confused, next to the chair, uncertain what was expected of her.

"Why does the old gwah lo man hold the chair?" she asked sheepishly. "I promise not to break it."

Lillian burst out into laughter, while her reserved manservant fought hard to hold back his laughter as well.

"What a delightful young lady you are," Lillian said. "John is only pulling the chair out for you as a courtesy. Please sit. John will push the chair closer to the table for you," she explained.

Still ravenous, Anna eagerly consumed a tall stack of pancakes swimming in heavy syrup and butter.

Gish placed a comforting hand on Anna's hand. "Child, it is now time that I know your situation. I assume you were not kidnapped by gypsies and managed to escape. Allow me to venture a wild guess. You got into an argument with your parents over something, and to spite them you ran away to join the circus," she voiced, half joking, half serious.

Anna's cheeks were puffed out like a chipmunk, filled with pancakes. She took a huge gulp of milk to wash down her breakfast. Coughing as she struggled to swallow her food, she sputtered, "Mrs. Gish my parents do not understand me. They are from Old China. I am not joining the circus, I want to be a famous actress."

"My dear child, I was only guessing about the circus part." Gish held out her coffee cup high, as a toast. "Anna May Wong, I toast you and your future acting career. I too am an actress. The silly profession has made me quite rich and famous. I am not married. I found it necessary to choose between a demanding husband and equally demanding children and being an actress, and I chose the latter." She smiled. "Child, please address me as Auntie Lilly. But first, before you obtain fame and fortune, I must take you home. I will speak on your behalf."

Anna's eyes widened and her mouth dropped open. "Lillian Gish! Shit! Now I remember where I have seen you — in flickers! You are a famous movie star!"

The doting Gish asked Anna to sit closer to her. "Dear girl, you must choose your words carefully. Famous actresses never curse — at least in public. Where did you learn the 'S' word?"

"Sorry Miss...uh, Auntie Lilly. I used to have a gwah lo friend and he often spoke the 'S' word and other swear words."

"Anna, your former friend is quite uncouth. It is good you two are no longer friends. So tell me, which of my 'flickers' did you enjoy the most?" asked Gish.

Anna had to think about it awhile, being that she had seen a great number of her films. "I liked *Way Down East* and *Birth of a Nation*," Anna replied.

Gish kissed Anna on her forehead. "Dear girl, those two were some of my favorites. In *Down East*, I refused a stunt double when I floated helplessly on that block of ice. My right hand dangled in the ice-cold water, and to this day my right hand still grows numb on certain days. As for *Birth of a Nation*, I have mixed feelings. It was the first big motion picture, beautifully filmed with several technical innovations, but being seventeen at the time, not much older than you now, I had no inkling the picture had racial overtones. But now that I am nearly thirty, I see that *Nation* portrayed the negroes as no better than savage beasts, while the superior white people — or gwah los, as your people call us — are God's gift to the world, and it's our destiny to rule with a heavy hand over the dark races of the world. What nonsense." She paused. "Child, when you think of *Birth of a Nation*, only think of my inspiring performance and not the film's message," encouraged Gish.

Anna did not at first understand Gish's negative view of the film. To her, it was an exciting adventure story. Being only ten when she saw it, she didn't know it was a harsh statement on white superiority. After a long moment of thought, she realized that the gwah lo's hateful snobbery was not exclusive to the yellow race she belonged to, but rather encompassed anyone who was different in appearance or belief.

"Hector, bring the car around," Gish ordered the chauffeur. "You're going home, Anna May Wong," quipped Gish as she grasped Anna's hand.

Anna's hand was perspiring heavily. "Auntie Lilly, I am afraid to face my parents."

"Anna dear, of course you're frightened. My kid sister Dorothy and I also dreamed of acting careers when we were very young. Like your parents, they strongly disapproved. We often had heated arguments with our parents, but just because Dorothy and I butted heads with our mother and father didn't mean we didn't love each other. I am certain your parents love you and you love them. Do not worry, my child. Auntie Lilly will smooth it out for you."

Anna nodded, feeling less anxious after hearing Gish's assuring words. Walking hand-in-hand with Gish, she was quite impressed with the grand mansion Gish lived in.

"Auntie Lilly, your house is so beautiful. Someday I will have a house as grand as yours."

Gish laughed, quite amused. "My dear child, my home is nothing but a pile of wood and stone. Your aspirations should be even grander. Someday I will show you my colleague and friend's mansion. Mary Pickford's home makes my home look like one of the dilapidated shacks the negroes lived in, in *Birth of a Nation*."

Anna felt special and important as she glided along the burgeoning city of Los Angeles in a chauffeur-driven Rolls Royce while sitting beside a famous movie star.

The sleek black automobile stopped in front of Sam Sing's Laundry. Lee You stepped outside, seemingly unimpressed by the luxury automobile. "Sir, today we are closed. We have a family emergency. Take your dirty laundry to the laundry on Willow Street," spoke Lee You to the chauffeur.

"Mrs. Wong, I am not bringing you dirty laundry, but rather I am returning your prodigal daughter," said Gish.

Gazing at the back seat, Lee You was startled to see her daughter sitting beside a gwah lo woman of obvious significance. "Liu Tsong! Your father and I have been worried to death about you." Lee You attempted to open the car door.

"Mrs. Wong, please allow the chauffeur to open the door. That is his job."

Anna's mother held out her arms to welcome her daughter home. Hesitantly, Anna allowed her mother to embrace her. "Mama, my name is Anna May, not Liu Tsong."

"What is happening?" queried Sam Sing as he emerged from the laundry.

"This kind lady has returned Anna to us," responded Lee You.

Sam Sing struck his daughter hard across the cheek. "Insolent brat! Do you realize how much worry you caused your mother? I told your mother not to worry, that you would return once your stomach began to rumble, but I was wrong. You shame your mother and me in front of this gwah lo lady."

Gish grimaced but did not protest immediately. She instead extended a friendly hand to Sam Sing. "Mr. Wong, I presume." She turned to Lee You. "And Mrs. Wong, I presume. Allow me a proper introduction. I am Lillian Gish."

"My apologies, Mrs. Gish, if my wayward daughter caused you any grief," voiced Sam Sing.

Lillian giggled. "Your excellent daughter was no trouble to me. My only regret is that Anna is not my own daughter. Incidentally, I am not married. Please call me Lilly or Miss Gish. And if I may please offer some advice, Anna May suits her. Liu Tsong, as pleasant a name as it is, does not have a memorable ring to it. If she is to succeed in the acting profession, Anna May is more suitable." She smiled. "Furthermore, Mr. Wong, if I may offer additional advice, slapping Anna May was not necessary. There are other ways to punish a child than to cause them physical pain."

Sam Sing glared at Gish with contempt. "You foolish gwah lo woman. Who are you to give advice? You have no children and no husband. Only prostitutes are actresses!" he screamed.

Gish laughed. "Mr. Wong, I am not a whore. I am one of the most respected actresses in America."

Sam Sing appeared quite shocked to hear that such a petite woman, who stood barely five feet tall, was a movie actress.

Gish, even more shockingly, embraced Sam Sing, kissing him on the cheek. "My sincere apologies, Mr. Wong. I have played too many strong, fearless heroines who do not take horse manure from anyone. I am too outspoken for my own good."

Sam Sing began cursing the impertinent gwah lo redhead. He opened the back door of the Rolls. "You have done your good deed for the day by bringing Liu Tsong home. Now go."

Lee You pulled Sam Sing to one side. "Husband, this gwah lo is a famous actress. I remember the workers speaking of her after returning from the Nickelodeon. She can make trouble for us. Perhaps she has friends in government who will close the laundry down," voiced Lee You in Chinese.

Sam Sing looked away for a moment, reflecting on his lifelong hatred and distrust of the gwah los. He remembered the time he was assaulted, and the gwah lo thugs stole a month's earnings, and how the gwah lo police ignored his pleas to investigate the crime against him.

"All right, wife. I will play the game to keep my business and put food in our mouths," said Sam Sing in Chinese. He turned to shake Gish's hand. "Miss Gish, I am a rude, stubborn man. I apologize for my rudeness. Thank you for returning Liu Tsong to us."

"Anna is such a lovely child. I would have been so honored to have her as my daughter. Please come to my home for coffee and cake. Hector will come pick up all three of you on Sunday — the day your laundry is closed — say, around noon. Yes? Good. See you Sunday," spoke a giddy Gish before Sam Sing and Lee You could respond.

The Wongs watched the Rolls Royce speed away.

"I was wrong. Gwah los do invite Chinamen for coffee and cake. And I do not even like coffee," voiced Sam Sing under his breath.

Anna gleefully jumped with joy. "Oh, Father, Mother! Please, let us go to Auntie Lilly's home for coffee and cake. She is the most wonderful lady I have ever met."

"What is this bullshit? You have only known this redheaded gwah lo a single day, and already you are addressing her as Auntie?" exclaimed Sam Sing.

"Husband, this Miss Gish has already explained, Anna is the daughter she never had," interjected Lee You.

"Let that gwah lo spinster buy a child. She has enough money to buy all the orphans in China."

Anna backed away from her parents. Anger and determination were clearly written on her face. "Father, Mother, I am fourteen years old. Nearly a grown woman. Please unlock the cage you've placed me in. I want to be an actress. If you think my future work makes me a lady of the evening, then so be it," voiced the outspoken Anna.

Sam Sing stormed into his laundry to search for his hidden whiskey bottle without responding to his daughter's ultimatum.

Lee You hugged Anna as tears rolled down her cheeks. "Anna, do not think bad thoughts about your father. It is not easy being a yellow man on the Gold Mountain. The gwah los have been mean to him all his life. He does not feel worthy of us. He is a beaten man, but despite his suffering, your father has worked hard to provide a roof over our heads and food for his family."

"Mother, I understand that he has suffered, but it is not my fault. Papa has never shown me any love. I will someday be a famous actress. The gwah los will pay money to see me in movies, and then the gwah los will respect my father. You, my mother, and all Chinese will worship me as they now worship Auntie Lilly," boasted Anna confidently.

"Of course we will, my daughter," spoke Lee You with a forced smile. "You rest now. It has been a hard day. I will speak to your father. I would be honored to have coffee and cake with your new redheaded aunt."

Lee You advised Anna to go to her bedroom to nap a bit, then work on her long-neglected school studies.

Upon entering Sam Sing's office to speak with him, she was disappointed to see her husband already feeling the effects of the whiskey he was quickly consuming. Sam Sing was leaning back in his swivel chair, his eyes glazed over. His face had turned a glowing red, a common trait of Asians who consumed too much liquor.

"No!" was Sam Sing's single-word response before Lee You even spoke.

"Yes," spoke the wife in an equally abbreviated manner.

"Yes, what?" asked Sam Sing.

Lee You snatched the bottle from Sam Sing's hand. "Husband, you know what 'yes' I am talking about just as I know what your 'no' meant. Sunday you and I and our daughter Anna, Liu Tsong, or whatever you wish to call her, will go to Miss Gish's home. Anna is right. She is nearly a grown woman and you've not said a kind word to her ever. For once in your daughter's life, do one thing on her behalf."

Sam Sing stood up. Struggling to stay upright, he shoved the cork forcefully into the whiskey bottle spout that Lee You held in her hand. "You win. One good deed for my disrespectful daughter," he said in a slurred voice.

5

On Sunday, the sleek black Rolls came to Sam Sing's Laundry precisely at noon, as Gish said it would. Anna was wearing the expensive blue dress Gish had gifted her. Her mother was wearing her only formal outfit — a glossy black, silk Asian-style dress — while her father wore the only suit he owned — a black suit and tie that he had not worn since the day of his wedding to Lee You.

Gliding through Los Angeles, Chinatown, and other districts, Lee You and Anna waved and shouted to Chinese acquaintances and customers of Sam's laundry, who watched the Wongs with disbelief and jealousy.

"Driver, honk your horn! There's that snooty Mrs. Hong Wing. Please honk to get her attention," spoke a very giddy Lee You.

"Shit, my wife and daughter, you act as if you are the dowager and her chief eunuch. You eat up those quick head-turns like hundred-dollar bird's nest soup."

"Husband, let me be the dowager for this one day, then I will return to washing the gwah los' soiled laundry."

The Rolls Royce turned onto a private, palm-tree-lined driveway. A giant, gray-stone mansion resembling the country home of a lord in the British countryside loomed before them. At the front entrance stood a grinning black man, who eagerly opened the door to the Rolls the moment it came to a halt.

"Welcome, Mr. and Mrs. Wong and daughter, to the Gish House. My name is Jonathan. Miss Gish will receive you in the garden."

"Hah!" whispered Sam Sing to his wife. "A hak gwai servant!

24

The gwah los think that is all the blacks and yellow people are good for — that and removing grease spots from their fine clothes."

"Mother, Father, Auntie Lilly's house is so beautiful," voiced an excited Anna as they walked, escorted by the black servant, through the immense interior of the home, eyeing the grand crystal chandeliers, original paintings with elaborately carved frames covered with gold guild, and beautiful furniture.

Upon entering the garden, the Wongs were even further awed by the thousands of beautiful flowers and trees.

Gish ran forward with open arms. She was purposely dressed in a silk, Chinese-styled robe. With cordial sincerity, Gish hugged Anna, kissing her on the forehead, then Anna's mother, and lastly, her father.

"Welcome, my dear, newfound friends. Please, come sit by the pool," invited Gish.

On a mahogany table sat a white sheet cake. In red frosting was written in Chinese the popular symbol meaning "double happiness." Fine blue china and two silver pots sat on the table as well, and bottled beer sat chilling in a silver ice bucket.

"Please sit, honored guests," Gish said warmly.

"Miss Gish, I have never seen such magnificent clothes," remarked Lee You. Gish spun around. "*Xie xie.* I believe in your language that means thank you, yes? I am pleased you like it. It is an exact replica of royal garments worn by your dowager, Empress Tzu-hsi."

With a green envy, Lee You sat, along with Sam Sing, Anna, and Gish.

"Being Chinese, I was uncertain whether you preferred coffee or tea, so I have both."

"Yes, Miss Gish, I would prefer a hot cup of tea. I have never developed a taste for the gwah lo drink coffee," stated Lee You, feeling uncomfortable in the ostentatious surroundings.

"Mindy, pour Mrs. Wong some tea. Oh dear, I am forgetting my manners. And fetch Anna a cold glass of milk," ordered Gish.

Anna quickly poured coffee into her cup and just as quickly drank the hot liquid, burning her tongue in the process. Ignoring the pain, she continued to drink the black coffee — a beverage Anna actually did not like, but drank nonetheless to give the appearance of maturity. "Auntie Lilly, forget the milk. That is a refreshment for children and I am a young woman," Anna said.

"Indeed you are, my child," responded Gish.

The moment held a thick air of awkwardness for both the Wongs and Gish. Sam Sing had not spoken a word since arriving. He turned his cup upside down on the saucer, indicating that he was not interested in coffee or tea.

"Mr. Wong, you strike me as a man who prefers his drink with more bite to it," Gish observed. "Mindy, pour Mr. Wong a glass of Double Happiness beer."

Sam's mouth dropped. "Where did you find this expensive Chinese beer? I've looked all over Los Angeles for it," he queried, amazed.

The maid poured a beer into a tilted glass so as not to give it too much of a foamy head.

Gish laughed. "I have a friend at the Chinese embassy in San Francisco. The dear ambassador sends me a case of the tasty Chinese beer every so often."

Sam Sing snatched the glass from the maid the moment she had poured the last drop from the bottle. He heartily drank the fine beer in what appeared to be a single, long swallow.

"The Chinese ambassador sends costly beer to a redheaded gwah lo, but not to a yellow brother who runs a lowly laundry," spoke Sam Sing in Chinese.

With forced politeness, Gish and her guests ate cake and drank their beverages in silence. Finally, to break the tension, Gish pulled some stapled papers from a leather a satchel that sat beside her lawn chair.

"Dear friends, I want to surprise you with something special. I have in my hands a couple of copies of Shakespeare's immortal play

Romeo and Juliet. In your honor, Mr. and Mrs. Wong, Anna and I will read an excerpt from this classic love story. I will play Romeo!" laughed Gish. "And your budding actress daughter Anna will play my lover, Juliet."

"What is this nonsense? Who the hell is Shakespeare and what is *Romeo and Juliet?"* asked Sam Sing.

"Husband, he is a great gwah lo writer, and *Romeo and Juliet* is a classic love story. The gwah lo missionaries told me so when I was a girl, before my parents and I immigrated to the Gold Mountain and I married a pig-headed Chinaman," exclaimed Lee You.

"Mr. Wong, it will be fun. Plus, I want to see if Anna has the heart of an actress."

Deeply agitated, Sam Sing ordered the maid to open another bottle of beer for him. "All right. My daughter never listens to me anyway. She does whatever she wishes." He snorted. "Such stubbornness. I don't know where she gets it," he added in frustration.

"Excellent. Anna and I will perform act two, scene two."

As the maid began to pour a second beer into a glass for Sam Sing, he snatched the bottle from the maid's hand and began guzzling directly from the bottle. Consuming the entire bottle in only a few gulps, he then flung the empty bottle onto the manicured lawn. "Miss Gish, I am ready to watch your fairy tale," spoke Sam Sing.

Gish rolled her eyes at the man's ill manners, but had no comment. She handed Anna a copy of the play, pointing to her lines on the page. She then instructed Anna to stand on a large, decorative boulder.

"Ladies and gentlemen, I give you *Romeo and Juliet,* authored by the greatest playwright of all time, William Shakespeare, starring Miss Anna May Wong as Juliet and Miss Lillian Gish as Romeo. In this scene we are about to perform, Juliet is at a second-story window, bidding her newfound lover Romeo good-bye."

Gish stood at the base of the boulder, gazing at Anna like a young man smitten by a young girl. "But, soft! What light through yonder window breaks? It is the east, and Juliet is the sun. Arise, fair sun, and kill the envious moon…" spoke Gish as Romeo.

Anna in return gazed down at Gish, very much absorbed by the character she was pretending to be. "O Romeo, Romeo! Wherefore art thou, Romeo?" voiced Anna, acting as if she were a girl deeply in love with a young boy her family would forbid her to see. "Good night, good night! Parting is such sweet sorrow, that I shall say good night till it be morrow," said Anna in the closing scene.

When Gish spoke her last words of dialogue, she climbed the boulder and kissed Anna softly on the lips.

"Bitch! How dare you kiss my teenage daughter!" screamed Sam Sing as he stormed toward Gish, shaking his fists.

Acting swiftly, Lee You slipped between her husband and Gish. "Dear husband, are you a fool as well as stupid? What Miss Gish did is called *acting*. Miss Gish did not kiss our daughter — *Romeo* kissed a girl named *Juliet,* who he is strongly in love with."

Sam Sing laughed insanely. "Hah! So you say, or maybe it was an excuse for her to kiss our daughter."

He attempted to strike Gish, but was stopped when the Jonathan, the butler, reacted by grabbing Sam Sing's arms from behind.

"Son-of-a-bitch! Hak gwai, let me go!" shouted Sam Sing. Struggling, he managed to break free, but lost his balance in the process and fell into the swimming pool.

"Help! Help! I can't swim!" pleaded Sam Sing, splashing wildly.

"Rescue Mr. Wong," ordered Gish, grinning wryly.

"Sorry…us hak gwais can't swim either," said Jonathan.

Acting instinctively, Anna dove into the pool to her father, pulling him to the safety of the edge. Jonathan lifted him out of the pool like a soggy bag of potatoes.

Sing fought to breathe as the butler placed him on his stomach on the lawn. Jonathan sat on him and aggressively pumped his hands on the half-drowned man's back.

Sam Sing coughed up a great deal of pool water. When it appeared he had no more water to cough up, Jonathan flipped him over.

"Mindy, send for the doctor," ordered Gish.

"No, damn it, I am not injured," Sing snarled. "Even if I did swallow half your swimming pool. I'm fine."

"Very well. Johnathan, assist Mr. Wong to a guest bedroom, draw him a hot bath, and provide some fresh clothes for him. Mindy, please do the same for Anna, and have her mother accompany her. Then have the ladies relax in the drawing room." She stood. "I will be with you ladies shortly, after I have a word with Mr. Wong."

A short time later, after Gish felt Sam Sing had had sufficient time to recoup from nearly drowning, she entered the guest bedroom without knocking.

"What is this?" Sing protested. "Gwah los do not believe in knocking before entering?" He sat in a padded leather chair sipping cognac.

"Mr. Wong, are you enjoying my fifty-year-old cognac?"

"Somewhat tasty. I like it about as much as I like this fancy suit your hak gwai flunky provided me." Sam Sing took a final sip of the fine liquor, set the glass on the side table, then stood up. "Miss Gish, I am ready to go home now. Please have your driver take me and my family home." He began to remove the exquisitely tailored jacket. "Give me back my clothes. I will wear them, wet or not."

Gish pulled the jacket back onto his torso, buttoned it, then pushed the man back into the leather chair. "Keep the suit. It used to belong to a gentleman friend who is no longer welcome at the Gish home."

She placed the glass back into Sam Sing's hand and poured a generous portion of cognac. Appearing to be agitated, the petite woman paced back and forth, glaring at Sam Sing. She then sat on the edge of the bed and poured herself some cognac. "Mr. Wong, you and I are two different people, but we need to make peace with one another. All I want is for your daughter to live a good and fruitful life. It's not fair for you or anyone to hold her back. Let me breathe life into her. Allow me to nurture her acting skills. I want

Anna to come live with me on the weekends. I will teach her the art of acting. I beg you, Mr. Wong, do not allow Anna to waste her life," she pleaded.

Sam Sing gulped down the cognac. His eyes burned with contempt. "Miss Gish—"

"Call me Lilly."

"Miss Gish, what the hell do you care if a 'yellow nigger,' as some gwah los have called me, succeeds or not?"

Gish gulped down her cognac. "Mr. Wong, I admit to having selfish reasons for embracing Anna. I never had children and I never will. I suppose I see so much of myself in Anna. My strong-willed sister Dorothy and I had our hearts set on being actresses. Our father wanted us to have a proper conventional life, to marry boys he had picked for us, and for us to bear many respectable children. Not that such a life is wrong, but it's not what Dorothy and I dreamed of. Mr. Wong, acting is not a silly or immoral profession any more than running a laundry is. They are both honorable professions."

Sam Sing reached his hand out, holding his glass. "Miss Gish...uh, Lilly... may I have a few drops more of your fifty-year-old cognac?" he asked in a softer tone.

Gish poured the glass nearly full. Sam Sing leaned back in the comfortable leather padded chair. Guzzling the hard drink down, he slammed the empty glass onto the nightstand. He then buried his face in his hands and began to sob. "I am an ugly little yellow man. Do what you want with Anna, I do not care."

Gish placed a kind hand on Sam Sing's shoulder. "I know you have been humiliated and hurt, and yes, it is so unfair that you and other people of color cannot be treated as equals. Perhaps the day will come when they will only see a beautiful girl with a beautiful soul. I don't know. Please allow Anna to cut a path to a level playing field for girls of color who will follow her. Give Anna to me for a while, and I will help her be Anna May Wong, actress. Which is not bad."

Gish leaned down to embrace Sam Sing and kissed him on the

cheek.

"Very well, Lilly, teach Anna to be white. I am too tired to fight any more battles. Let my daughter fight the good fight," said Sam Sing.

Gish smiled coolly. "Sam, if I may call you Sam, you are a cynical, bitter man. I will teach Anna to act and survive in a competitive profession, but to be white...that I cannot do."

6

The following weekend, the Rolls stopped in front of Sam Sing Laundry promptly at nine in the morning. Anna was standing outside on the sidewalk with a weathered suitcase in hand. Jonathan greeted her with a cordial, "Good morning," and like a proper chauffeur, held the door for Anna to enter the vehicle.

While cruising toward Gish's mansion, Anna eyed four gwah lo girls who frequently bullied her in school.

"Bitches. They think they're so much better than me," spoke Anna out loud.

"Miss Anna, those honky young ladies been picking on you?" asked Jonathan.

Anna nodded her head shyly.

"Well, damn, Miss Anna. It's time we knock them honky brats off their high horses."

The chauffeur honked loudly as the shiny vehicle passed the girls.

"Don't forget to wave and smile at your friends as we pass, Missy Anna."

Doing as she was told, Anna waved and grinned widely at her tormentors. The schoolgirls gawked at Anna and the luxury auto she rode in with shock and envy. Anna began to giggle, and clapped her hands with giddy pleasure. For the first time in her life, she felt special.

As the Rolls arrived at the Gish mansion, Lillian was at the entrance with open arms. She embraced Anna as warmly as any mother greeting her daughter after a long absence.

"No time to waste, young lady," said Gish as they walked arm-in-arm across the Italian-marble hallway to the spacious gardens. They stood together beside the actress's Olympic-sized swimming pool, and Gish whispered into Anna's ear, "Do not fear the future, my beloved child. Too many people fail because they are more afraid of success than failure. Be bold and amazing. Be fearless my —"

Before Gish could finish her sentence, the chauffeur surprised them by leaping out of the bushes. He was brandishing a large, wicked revolver.

"Missy Gish, I am tired of begging for scraps at your dinner table. Instead of begging for chump change, why not kill my snooty mistress and take all of it?" stated Jonathan in an angry, vindictive voice.

Gish shoved Anna behind her and laughed insanely. "You sniveling, cowardly negro, you haven't got the guts to kill a mongrel dog let alone a great movie star such as me."

As Gish continued to laugh, the servant repeatedly fired the .38 caliber pistol until he had fired all six rounds the gun contained.

Gish fell to the ground, clutching her chest. "Oh, Jonathan, how could you!" she cried as she closed her eyes, her body going limp.

Tears rushed down Anna's face. She leaped toward the black servant, disregarding her own safety. "You damn hak gwai! Auntie Lilly was like my second mother, bastard!" she screamed, slamming her fists against the man's chest.

"Anna dear, stop striking Jonathan. Good help is hard to find," spoke a voice she had not expected to hear again.

Turning around, Anna was startled to see Gish standing behind her, very much alive. "Auntie Lilly...you're alive!"

Gish pulled a monogrammed silk handkerchief from her sleeve to wipe away Anna's tears. "My apologies, my young friend. This is your first acting lesson. Sometimes it's more important to *react* than act."

Anna was confused. "Auntie Lilly...you're not dead...or hurt?"

Gish and Jonathan laughed.

"Child, Jonathan has been with me for five years. He would give his life for me. The dear man was shooting blanks. It's called play acting. When the camera is rolling, you must become the character you are pretending to be to the point that it is no longer acting. If your Auntie Lilly is savagely killed, you must react as though I really had been shot," preached Gish.

Anna hugged Gish, relieved that what had occurred was not real. "Auntie Lilly, I have so much to learn."

"Welcome to showbiz, child," quipped Gish.

And so began Anna's grueling weekends of acting lessons. The gentle, petite redhead transformed into a demanding taskmaster.

"No, damn it! No vocal pauses," she would shout. "Damn it, Anna, you blink your eyes too much."

"Auntie Lilly, if the movies have no sound, what difference does it make how I speak?" queried Anna.

Gish clasped her hands upon Anna's cheeks, planting a kiss on her lips. "My beautiful child, you speak to feel the soul of the character you are portraying. It's not important that the audience hears your voice, only that *you* can hear it."

Every Saturday evening after dinner in Gish's mansion, the two would ride in the Rolls, chauffeured by Jonathan, to a nearby movie theater to watch the most currently released films. Later, they would get a late-night snack of dim sum in Chinatown. Then, they often talked late into the night in the mansion's drawing room, discussing the main characters' performances and the movie's plotline.

Without her parents' knowledge, Anna would frequently skip school to watch film crews shoot movies in the Los Angeles Chinatown area. At age fourteen, Anna was blossoming into a beautiful young woman. One day, as she often did, Anna climbed atop a high bronze Buddha statue for a clear view of a film being shot in Chinatown. As the film crew busily prepared the day's shoot, two security guards approached Anna.

Fearing she was in trouble, she leaped from the statue. The numerous bystanders, bunched together below her, broke her fall.

Amid the cursing fellow Chinese, Anna frantically ran down the street. But the fast-acting guards managed to overtake her.

"Please, sir, I will not climb atop the Buddha statue again. Let me go."

The guards chuckled. "Little girl, we haven't chased you down to admonish you. We work for the film's director. He wants to talk to you about appearing in his movie. Are you interested?" asked one of the guards.

Anna was dumbfounded by the offer. "Oh, yes! Yes! I want to be in a flicker."

Escorted by the guards, Anna was led to a man sitting in a canvas folding chair and barking orders through a megaphone. He was a middle-aged man sporting a thick mustache with an athletic build, who appeared to be accustomed to giving orders.

"Ah, Miss Anna Wong, I am deeply honored. Allow me to introduce myself. I am Chase Lawrence, the director of *The Red Lantern*," stated Lawrence as he kissed her hand.

"How did you know my name, Mr. Lawrence?"

The director flashed an uncomfortable look in response to her question.

"Uh, uh...L.A.'s Chinatown is a small community. All the Orientals here know everybody. I simply asked if anyone knew who that gorgeous China girl was sitting atop that statue," responded Lawrence glibly. "In any case, my dear, it is not important how I determined your name. What is important is that you appear in my movie. You are perfect for the role of Ling Sue. The role pays fifty dollars a week. Do you accept?"

Anna screamed in ecstasy, "Yes! Yes!" She wrapped her arms around the director.

"Very good. Here is the script. Unfortunately, technology has not yet invented movies with sound, but you will need to learn the nature of each scene you will appear in. Arrive at the set tomorrow at six a.m. And be prompt."

Intoxicated with euphoria, Anna ran home barefoot, her shoes removed to enable her to run faster. When she arrived at her father's laundry, she dashed up the stairs to the family's living quarters. "Papa! Mama! I am a real actress! I start tomorrow my first acting job! Mama, Papa I am so deliriously happy!" exclaimed Anna as she spun around and around with excitement.

Lee You appeared quite joyful at her daughter's glamorous new job, while Sam Sing's face appeared skeptical.

"Daughter, how exactly did you find this generous offer of fame and riches?" queried her father with coldness in his voice.

"Papa, the director saw me sitting atop the bronze Buddha in Chinatown. He said I am gorgeous and perfect for the part, and he said I am to be paid fifty dollars a week!"

Sam Sing threw his arms up in the air. "This gwah lo 'important man' saw you sitting on a statue and decided to make you a famous movie celebrity, and you will be paid fifty dollars a week? More money than I sometimes earn in one week running my laundry? It is obvious to me this gwah lo son-of-a-bitch just wants to pleasure himself with an underage Chinese girl."

Lee You pounded her arm on the table. "Husband," she spoke under her breath in Chinese, "to act in a movie is a great honor. You need to show your daughter encouragement. Besides, do you not think if this gwah lo director wanted to bed a young Chinese girl, he could find one for far less than fifty dollars a week?"

"Very well," whispered Sam Sing. "Daughter, I congratulate you on your first real job. It is certainly more profitable than the pennies I pay you to fold and iron clothes in my laundry. Good luck, my daughter. Make your fellow Chinese proud of you," voiced Sam Sing as he hugged Anna one of the few times in her life.

After her father's embrace, Anna then hugged her mother, then turned to rush out the door.

"Anna, where are you going? Dinner is almost ready," asked her mother.

"Mama, I am not hungry. I must tell Auntie Lilly the good news!"

Anna jumped on her bicycle and raced the five miles to Gish's mansion.

It was full darkness when Anna arrived. Anna frantically pounded on the front door until the maid opened it.

"Missy Wong, what brings you here at this hour?" asked the maid.

"Mindy, it's all right," Gish said. "Let me visit with my little friend in private. Bring us hot tea in the study." She led Anna into the study. "Please sit. Now, child, tell me...what is so important that you could not wait until this weekend to inform me of?"

Anna tried to catch her breath. "Auntie Lilly, I am going to act in my first movie. I start tomorrow!"

Gish motioned with her hands for Anna to come sit next to her. Gish held Anna as tightly as if she were her own daughter. "Anna, my child, I am so proud of you! Oh, how I wish you were my daughter."

Anna and Gish's eyes met with mutual admiration and affection.

"Oh, Aunt Lilly, I am your daughter. My parents never wanted me."

Gish shook her harshly. "Don't say that, my child. They love you, but they have their own demons to battle, especially your father. Someday, when you're older, you will understand. But enough of this sentimentality, Anna. We have work to do. Let me see the script. I will teach you all I know to make your debut a memorable one."

Gish rang a bell that was sitting on the mantle. Jonathan soon appeared. "Jonathan, drive to the Wong residence at once. Inform Mrs. Wong she will prepare a night bag for Anna. She is spending the night with me. Oh, and tell Anna's parents not to worry. She is in good hands. I am tutoring their daughter to become the world's first and foremost female Asian movie star."

"Yes, madam, I am on my way."

Gish then commanded two of her other servants to push all the furniture in the study against the walls. "We need open space to practice your scenes, my dear," voiced Gish as she carefully studied the script. "Ah good...ah good...interesting..." mumbled Gish as she read the script over and over.

Gish placed Anna in the center of the room.

"Anna, you are now Ling Sue. It is 1900. You are a lady of the evening. The Chinese Boxers are battling the foreigners to drive the white devils out of China, and you are madly and insanely in love with one of the Boxer rebels. A British soldier savagely kills your lover. Bang! Bang!" screamed Gish, pretending to fire a pistol, her index finger the gun barrel and her thumb the gun hammer. "Bang! Bang!" again she cried. Gish fell to the floor. "I am your lover, who has just been fatally shot. Now, Anna...how do you react?"

"Cry?" asked Anna.

"No, that makes it too easy. It must be more. You remember the subtle blend of sadness and anger you felt when you thought Jonathan had shot me dead?"

Anna nodded.

"Now, show me something that will reach down and touch something inside of me, my child."

Anna fought back the tears. She reached down and kissed Gish gently on her lips. With fire in her eyes, she rose up and began pounding the chest of an imaginary British soldier. "Gwah lo bastard, take me! Take me! I have nothing else to live for."

"Bravo! Bravo!" shouted Gish as she stood up, clapping with gusto.

Into the wee hours, Gish and Anna rehearsed her scenes over and over. At two-thirty, Gish ordered Anna to bed.

Anna had only a few hours of fitful sleep. Gish awakened her with hot tea and her favorite Chinese pastries, dim sum.

"Auntie Lilly, you did not give me much time to rest before my special day."

"Exactly, my dear. You need a hard edge. You need to be in a desperate place. That is the character you are portraying."

Together, Anna and her mentor rode to the film set. Though the sun hadn't yet risen, the film crew had already been working a couple of hours, preparing the set with high-wattage lights and props.

The director smiled when he saw Gish. "Lilly, Lilly, the love of my life! We haven't made a movie together in two years. Are you avoiding me?" joked the film director as he ran with open arms to embrace her.

"Chase, you naughty boy. I am too much of a woman for you to handle."

"Ah, you have brought me the next 'big thing,' Miss Anna May Wong."

Anna reached out to shake hands with Mr. Lawrence. "Mr. Lawrence, I am so—"

But before she could complete her sentence, the director turned his back to her, whispering into Gish's ear, "Lilly, dear girl, this yellow tart better not screw up my big-budget flick. You owe me big time if she does. I'm doing you a big favor."

Gish glared at Lawrence contemptuously, "Anna is Chinese, not a yellow tart, and she will not let you down," she said through clenched teeth.

Though Lawrence and Gish did not think Anna heard their conversation, she had keen ears and heard every word. She was crushed at the realization that Gish had arranged everything.

Finally turning his attention to Anna, the director said, "Miss Wong, go with this lady. She will take you to wardrobe to dress you in the clothes of the character you are playing."

Gish embraced her tightly. "Anna, my love, you will set the world on fire. Fear not. You are a fearless woman warrior. Be strong. Be bold." With an encouraging smile, Gish left the set.

Anna had hoped Auntie Lilly would stay to watch her performance, but she had told her on the ride to the set that she might be too much of a distraction if she stayed.

After several minutes in wardrobe and several more minutes in make-up, Anna stepped reluctantly onto the film set. She was wearing a very revealing, low-cut dress with face make-up so heavy it was almost clown-like. She was startled to see some five hundred

Chinese extras on the set.

"Miss Wong, you look so divine," spoke Lawrence. "Allow me to introduce to you your love interest, Lao Ping."

Anna eyed the actor with confusion and discomfort. Standing before her was a six-foot-tall gwah lo man with blue eyes.

"But Mr. Lawrence, this man is a gwah lo."

"A what?" asked the director impatiently.

"This is a white man. My lover is Chinese," stated Anna with a cutting tone.

The actor extended a friendly hand to Anna. "Pleased to meet you, Miss Wong. I am Dax Dortmunder."

Anna ignored the actor and his offer of a handshake.

"Miss Wong," the director said, "my expert make-up man has narrowed the white — uh...gwah lo gentleman's eyes. He may not be Chinese, but he looks very much like a Chinese," explained Lawrence glibly. "China girl, now get your ass ready for the first scene or Summit Studios will sue your parents for every yen they own."

Shocked, but fearful of Lawrence's threats, Anna said nothing in protest. Doing as she was told, Anna walked back and forth on the Chinatown sidewalk as the director ordered, "Action!"

Despondent, she paced with her head down, a sullen gaze on her face.

"Cut! Cut! Cut!" screamed Lawrence. "Damn it, China girl, you're supposed to be a lady of the evening. You look like someone just shoved a corncob up your ass. You need to act sensual. You need to act like you're God's gift to men. Smile! Hold your head up. Walk with a flirty gait. You got that, my yellow brat?"

Fighting a strong urge to strike Lawrence, Anna relented, "Yes, sir. I understand." She put aside in her mind the indignities and racial undertones. She wanted so much to be an actress.

She straightened her back and held her head up high. Her painted bright-red lips smiled widely at the gwah lo actor portraying the Chinese Boxer rebel. "You want good time, cute farm boy?" she said.

Though it was a silent film, the actors nonetheless spoke actual words in the script for dramatic effect.

The male actor returned the flirtatious smile. "Miss, you are very beautiful, but I am only a lowly country boy fighting to drive the greedy foreign devils from our Mother China. I am not worthy of you."

"Country boy, you are bravely risking your life to drive the white devils from China. There will be no charge. I am Ling Sue."

Anna took the young man by his arm and escorted him to her humble one-room flat. The rebel fighter had fallen in love with the fallen angel.

Anna's first film scene went well. As the plot developed, the prostitute Anna portrayed eventually grew to love the rebel farm boy as well.

Over the next few weeks, Anna put aside her resentment that her imaginary lover was a gwah lo pretending to be Chinese. Being true to her newfound profession, she became more and more absorbed in her role. Every night she was driven home in a chauffeur-driven Bugatti provided by the film studio.

With only the energy and giddiness a teenage girl could have, Anna would excitedly waltz into the upstairs living quarters of her home to share the details of each day's filming. She would always substitute her role as a "lady of the evening" with that of simply being the rebel boy's girlfriend.

It was questionable whether her parents had accepted their daughter's chosen profession. Gish's chauffeur Jonathan came to the family laundry almost every night, requesting that Anna speak with his mistress. Each time Anna declined the request to visit Gish, incensed that she had only gotten the film role because of the strings Gish pulled.

On the final day of shooting, Anna was faced with her most dramatic and challenging scene.

"Anna babe, this is your day of reckoning, to see if you have the

41

balls for this insane business or not. Your lover has just been killed by a British son-of-a-bitch soldier. You're obviously outraged. You lunge toward the asshole. The goddamn limey then shoots you. You fall to the ground, covered in blood. You crawl to your lover so you two can die in each other's arms. You got that, China doll?" directed Lawrence.

Anna nodded her head. "I understand, Mr. Lawrence."

A prop lady approached and poured a sticky black goo all over the front of her blouse.

"What is this?" cried Anna.

"My dear, it is chocolate syrup. It takes the place of blood. This is show biz, darling. You didn't think we would use real blood, did you?" spoke the prop woman with a sarcastic grin.

Anna smeared a dab of it with her finger and tasted the sweet concoction. "But...but it doesn't look like blood," voiced Anna.

"Honey, this movie is black and white. They ain't invented color moving pictures yet. The black syrup looks like the real thing. Besides, we get to eat it over ice cream during the breaks," chuckled the prop woman. "Oh, one last thing, cover your blouse with your jacket till the limey shoots you."

The crew frantically set up the scene and the director barked directions. Anna stood anxiously, speaking in silent words, *I will not fail, I will not fail, be strong, be strong.*

The climactic scene began with the director's usual single-word command, "Action!"

An epic, make-believe battle ensued. It was a re-enactment of the historic Boxer Rebellion where rebel Chinese fought to drive foreigners from China, as it was felt they were exploiting their country. Hundreds of Chinese rebel Boxers with uniformed soldiers from numerous nations marched on Peking to rescue their besieged diplomatic corps.

Lao Ping rushed forward, ahead of his comrades. A British soldier dropped him in a single shot to the heart. The make-believe rebels retreated from the overwhelming firepower.

"Cut!" yelled the director.

An assistant hurried to drip chocolate syrup on the fallen man's chest and mouth.

As ordered, Anna straddled her marker, waiting nervously for the camera to resume rolling. Again the director shouted, "Action!"

The chaotic retreat of the Boxers began. Anna's character pushed forward through those fleeing to reach her lover. "Oh, my sweet Lao Ping, please, I beg you, do not die. I cannot see my life without you," spoke Anna's character Ling Sue as she held Ping in her arms.

The man's eyes half opened and he gently touched Ling Sue's cheek, smearing the pretend blood on her face.

"Forgive me, my love, I cannot grant your request. I have given my life to China. Good-bye, my love. We will meet again someday," voiced the dying man as he slowly closed his eyes and exhaled his final breath.

Real tears flowed from Anna's eyes. "Yes, we will meet again, my love..." she whispered hoarsely.

The British soldier responsible for Lao Ping's death stood over the lovers, laughing mockingly.

With exaggerated sadness and anger, Anna's character lunged at Ping's killer. The soldier fatally shot Ling Sue without hesitation. With a determined will, Ling Sue crawled to her lover, collapsing atop her lover's body, joining him in death.

"Cut!" yelled the director.

The entire set erupted in applause over Anna's performance. "Bravo! Bravo!" was the collective cry from the film crew, many bystanders, and fellow actors.

Anna stood up and bowed with euphoric delight. The actor portraying Lao Ping joined Anna in bowing. Anna cursed the actor in Chinese for forcing his tongue into her mouth as they kissed, but the actor only smiled politely, believing that she was complimenting him in Chinese.

To her amazement and surprise, dozens of onlookers swarmed around her, asking for her autograph.

"As a yellow movie star, that's even more special than a dancing bear," whispered Dortmunder to an assistant.

As Anna returned home after the day's filming and autograph signing, she felt it was undoubtedly the happiest day of her life. Eager to tell her parents about the eventful day, she rushed into their upstairs residence, shouting at the top of her lungs, "Father, Mother! I've had the most wonderful day!"

To her astonishment, her parents displayed a cold stare toward their daughter's revelation.

"Anna dear, you acted in a movie and a good many people asked for your autograph. How nice," spoke her mother with glib sincerity.

"How did you know people asked for my autograph, Mother?"

"Daughter, your mother and I were in the crowd watching you pretend to be a lady of the evening. Is that what you want us to be proud of?" quipped Sam Sing.

"Anna, you told us you were the Boxer's girlfriend, not a soiled dove," stated Lee You.

Anna lowered her head in shame. She looked at her parents with sorrowful eyes. "You do not understand. It's pretend. Even Auntie Lilly played a lady of the evening. All my life people have ignored me. My parents ignore me."

Lee You stepped slowly toward her daughter and put her arms around Anna, pressing Anna's face against her chest. "My daughter, I am so sorry. I want to understand. Even our own people have shunned your father and me, disapproving of your acting. They think a Chinese girl's place is with her family at home, that she should marry well and bear her parents lots of grandchildren. Give your father and I time to get used to a journey no Chinese girl has ever taken."

Anna turned to her father for a response to her mother's words of encouragement. Sam Sing turned and walked into the bedroom, saying nothing more to his daughter.

Deeply dejected, Anna turned and ran down the stairs. Her mother stood at the landing, pleading for her daughter to return.

"Anna, my love, please come back! Your father will come around. Please, I beg you to be patient..."

7

Anna walked down the street with no idea where she would go or what she would do. A familiar Rolls Royce pulled up alongside her and an equally familiar voice called out her name.

"Anna, dear child, are you running away from home and your parents again? Please get in and tell Auntie Lilly what's wrong."

Anna ignored Gish's pleadings as she stomped down the street. The Rolls stopped. Jonathan leaped out of the car and blocked Anna's way.

"China girl, get in the Rolls. It's for your own good. If you don't, I will send the police after you and have you arrested as a runaway," threatened the hulking black chauffeur.

She stopped in her tracks, staring contemptuously at the man.

"Missy? Or worse, yet I will have the authorities arrest you for bad acting," quipped Jonathan.

Anna burst out laughing. "My acting is no worse than when you pretended to kill Miss Gish." With that said, Anna stepped into the back of the car and sat down beside Lilly.

As the Rolls started moving again, Lilly looked at Anna. "Anna, what is troubling you so? Your debut performance was lovely! Even the great Gish sisters could not have given a better performance."

"How do you know about my performance?" asked Anna.

"I saw it in the editing room. Now tell me...what is wrong, when everything is starting to go your way?"

Anna did not look at Gish, but rather gazed out the window at the passing scenery. "My parents were not proud of me. I did not tell

46

them I was going to play a lady of the evening...but what difference does it make if I become a major actress? I did not earn it. The great movie star Lillian Gish bought me the role. I did not earn it myself."

Gish smiled softly, shrugging her shoulders. "Child, everyone needs a hand up in the beginning. True, I opened the door for you, but only you, Anna May Wong, must have the courage and determination to step inside. A man named D.W. Griffith gave this inexperienced little redhead a chance to act in a movie called *Birth of a Nation*. I was only a couple of years older than you when I got the part. Certainly, it was a flawed film, degrading the negro, but it was my big break nonetheless. D.W. used his influence with the studio to get me the role. How is that any different from me putting in a good word for you?"

Anna closed her eyes, feeling no relief from Gish's reassuring words. "Auntie Lilly, I am not gwah lo. I am only a yellow dancing bear. I overheard the gwah lo actor who played my lover say as much."

"Damn that kraut's soul. Dortmunder was probably just jealous that you're a better actor. But if you are a dancing bear, yellow or any other color, for my people to accept people of color, it would take someone like Frederick Douglas fighting for the rights of the negroes, or Anna May Wong standing tall for the Chinese."

"Yes, I learned of Mr. Douglas in grade school. I do not have his strength. I wanted to be accepted by the gwah los, but now I only want to act. Good-bye, Auntie," murmured Anna as she opened the door and leaped out of the moving vehicle.

Anna rolled onto the street, sustaining only a few scrapes and bruises. She swiftly rose to her feet and disappeared into a stand of trees. For a number of minutes, Gish and her chauffeur pleaded loudly for Anna to return, but their pleas were ignored as Anna ran away and didn't look back.

Having run a great distance, she finally collapsed on a park bench. It was now dark. Anna was exhausted, hungry, and shivering from the nighttime ocean breeze. Anna was frightened and confused.

She thought of returning home or going to Gish's mansion, but such thoughts were quickly erased by her foolish pride.

I never win once. As a small child, my parents took me to the beach. The water was so warm and inviting...perhaps I should swim far out till I cannot swim anymore. It would not be such a bad way to die, thought Anna.

She shook her head, then said aloud to herself, "No, no, I will set the world on fire, like Auntie Lilly said. I want to live! To hell with the gwah los who look down on me. I will show them!"

Dozing off periodically, the cold prevented her from a deep sleep. When the chilly night became too unbearable, she paced back and forth, rubbing her arms to warm herself.

When the blessed sun finally rose in the east, Anna recalled the name of the film studio the director worked for. She eyed a postman delivering mail. The man kindly gave her directions to Summit Studios. Feeling sorry for the poor girl, the postman gave her thirty cents; a nickel for the trolley and a quarter to purchase a much-needed breakfast.

After consuming a hearty stack of pancakes and milk at a nearby café, Anna rode the trolley to Summit Studios. Upon arriving at the front entrance, Anna was quite surprised at the immenseness of the studio complex.

A guard manned the high, iron-gated entrance.

Anna looked quite unsightly in her tattered, soiled clothes and with bruises on her arms and legs.

"Stop!" cried the guard as Anna attempted to enter the studio grounds. "You little street tramp, if you're looking for a free meal, go to the soup kitchen downtown. Here, I'll write down the address for you."

After handing Anna a small scrap of paper with the address to the soup kitchen written on it, the guard smacked her on the rump. "Now get going, you trashy yellow brat."

Venting her anger after a hard day and night, Anna wadded the paper into a ball and threw it at the guard's face. "Gwah lo bastard! I am a big movie actress. I appeared in *The Red Lantern*. I am a star. I want to speak to my director, Mr. Lawrence."

The guard cackled with laughter. "Little girl, you expect me to believe that you acted in *The Red Lantern* and Mr. Chase Lawrence directed you? Let me introduce myself, I am President Woodrow Wilson," sneered the guard with cutting sarcasm.

In growing frustration, Anna kicked the guard in the shin. He cried out as Anna forcefully kicked the man's other shin, causing him to drop to his knees.

The guard managed to grab her arm, preventing her from fleeing. Both the man and the girl cursed at each other, the guard shouting in English and Anna cursing in Chinese.

"Hank, what the hell do you think you are doing?" exclaimed the film director Chase Lawrence.

The guard sprang to his feet, clearing his throat. "Mr. Lawrence...uh...uh...this bratty chink girl was trying to sneak into the studio compound. She gave me this ridiculous bullshit that she appeared in your latest movie. I was only doing my duty, Mr. Lawrence."

Lawrence lifted her into his arms. "Hank, how dare you strike my protégé. Miss Wong was magnificent in *The Red Lantern*. Pack your things and get the hell off studio property. You're fired!"

"Uh...uh...Mr. Lawrence, I didn't know this China girl was a friend of yours," explained the guard.

"Miss Wong isn't a friend. I told you, she is my protégé. She is more than a friend."

Lawrence looked at the downtrodden young girl in contemplative thought. "Miss Wong, having a difficult day?"

Giving no verbal response, she merely rolled her eyes with a subtle grin.

"Young lady, being a runaway, how far did you think you would get with no money, no food, no connections?"

Anna's eyes widened. "How did you know I ran away from home?"

"Girl, you look as if you've just wrestled with a mountain lion — a battle which you did not win. Why else would you be coming to see the most talented director in the world, Chase Lawrence?" He chuckled. "First things first. I'll take you to my home to clean you up, sort out what troubles you, and then I will have a chat with your parents."

"Mr. Lawrence, thank you. I could think of no one else to turn to."

"And your Auntie Lilly? Why did you not seek salvation from Miss Gish?"

"I no longer want to see Auntie Lilly. It is only because of her that you gave me the acting job in your movie."

Lawrence cackled. "What foolish pride for someone so young. Understand this, my silly Chinese diva. Yes, dear Lilly convinced me to hire you. But I would have fired your ass, whether my good friend Lilly recommended you or not, if I didn't think you were giving a good performance. In fact, you were spectacular in *The Red Lantern,* and I have more roles in mind for you."

Anna said nothing in response to Lawrence's reassuring words. Her mind was a muddled mess of confusion as to who she should trust or what words to believe.

They arrived at a mansion even more magnificent than Lillian Gish's. The chauffeur assisted Anna out of the limousine.

"You live here?" asked Anna in awe.

"It's home, but it's a mere outhouse compared to the palace owned by Mary Pickford and Douglas Fairbanks," stated Lawrence as he pointed a finger at the grand dwelling across the street. "They call it Pickfair. A rather quaint name, don't you think?"

An attractive blond around forty rushed out to greet them.

"Chase, my love, who is this odd little oriental girl?" asked the woman.

Lawrence placed protective hands on Anna's shoulders. "Priscilla, this lovely young lady is Anna May Wong. She is my protégé. I plan to groom her into the world's first female Asian motion-picture star. Anna my friend, allow me to introduce you to my faithful and always late wife, Priscilla," voiced Lawrence with a touch of animosity.

"Ha! Anna, pay no attention to my bullshitting husband. I am late only when I am required to meet Chase's stuffy studio investors from back east. My husband kisses their asses to bankroll his films, but I refuse to do that."

Lawrence cleared his throat. "Perhaps it's time for your evening bottle while I tend to Anna's welfare," he sneered with obvious sarcasm.

Pricilla stormed off.

"Come with me, Miss Wong," spoke Lawrence as he led Anna to a glass elevator.

Nervously, Anna stepped lightly into one of the mansion's guest bedrooms as Lawrence held open the door. The sleeping quarters were larger than Anna's parents' entire upstairs living space.

"Make yourself comfortable, young lady," said Lawrence, as he reached out to touch her.

Slapping away his hand, she grabbed a fire poker that was on a stand by the fireplace and held it out in front of her. "Auntie Gish warned me of gwah lo men who will try to have their way with me. Hear me out. You will be bedding a dead girl if you try."

Lawrence chuckled with delighted amusement. "Miss Wong, young ladies come on to me almost every day, hoping to get a role in one of my movies. If I desired to bed teenage bait, I could do so with much less trouble than making a pass at a high-strung Chinese girl."

Anna dropped the poker. "Why are you helping me?"

A sorrowful look grew on the man's face. Lawrence sat on a chair as if Anna's question was a blow to the head. He pulled a flask of brandy from his coat pocket and inhaled a long measure of the liquor.

"Lilly and I are close friends. She told me she has treated you with such generosity because you are the daughter she never had, and wishes she had. You are also the daughter I never knew. Fifteen years ago I was directing a film in London. Cilla was pregnant at the time. She begged me to stay and give her support as she gave birth to our first child, but being the son-of-a-bitch that I am, I left her side to direct what I felt would be a masterpiece. The critics and the public loved my movie, but in exchange for artistic glory, I was not beside Cilla when our daughter was stillborn. She did not breathe a single breath."

Lawrence took another gulp of brandy, then continued.

"She would have been your age had she lived. Like your Auntie Lilly, you are the daughter I never had. Because of health issues, Cilla can never bear another child.

Anna slowly approached Lawrence to embrace him. "Mr. Lawrence, we both know pain. I will act for you."

The director nodded his head. "Good. We have much to do. I will have the maid draw a hot bath for you. When you are refreshed, take a moment to read the stack of film ideas that are on the table over there." He nodded to a table in the corner of the room.

Feeling more at ease with the gwah lo director, Anna allowed him to kiss her hand before he left the bedroom.

The maid entered to draw her bath, then took Anna's clothes to be washed, ironed, and mended.

Placing her right toe in the bath water to test the temperature, Anna slowly descended into the warm, embracing bath. Her feet, covered in soap suds, playfully fondled the gold-plated bath fixtures. Steam drifted off the water as she closed her eyes, sliding down until only her head was visible above the sudsy water. She was nearing her fifteenth birthday, and like any girl of that age, felt a growing sensual urge. Outside of her father, there were few people of the opposite sex that she'd had contact with. She remembered Marion Morrison, nicknamed Duke — the first boy her same age she had befriended. She remembered him as being so tall and handsome, but whatever sexual desire she had felt for him soon faded. He had been more like a big protective brother, and she the little sister who needed protection.

"Who am I? Where am I going?" murmured Anna softly.

Being a virgin, she entertained the thought of sleeping with a man. She giggled, reflecting on how she had falsely believed that Lawrence had tried to make advances toward her. *Mr. Lawrence is not a bad looking man for someone so old,* thought Anna. *Would I really have fought him off had he tried to force himself on me? I will never know.*

Gently, she ran her right hand along her smooth right thigh. Thoughts of the many handsome male actors she had watched in hundreds of flickers flashed in her mind. She fought the urge to touch herself, and pulled her hand away, feeling guilty and embarrassed, as if the whole world was watching her.

After a long and soothing bath, she toweled herself dry, then covered her naked body with a luxurious white bathrobe. Upon entering the bedroom, she was impressed to see her clothes folded neatly on the edge of the bed. They had been thoroughly cleaned and pressed and the rips finely sewn.

She sat in a custom-carved chair reading the film plots Lawrence had left for her to review, and about the female characters she might play. She paged through the stack. "*The China Girl Temptation, The Bigwig of Chinatown...*" Anna shook her head with amused displeasure. "Not exactly stories equal to Shakespeare," she whispered to herself.

One story she found especially stereotypical was *The Shanghai Streetwalker.*

Shit, is there no role Mr. Lawrence has planned for me where I am not a lady of the evening? She removed her robe and stood before a full-length mirror, eyeing her slender, small-breasted body. She giggled at the irony that she had portrayed a prostitute, and perhaps would again in several similar roles to come, considering that, in real life, she was a virgin. She pondered what a young man of any race would think of her body. Would any yellow, white, or green boy ever desire such a body? "Damn China girls have such small tits," quipped Anna as she painfully pinched her nipples, hoping to make her breasts larger. "Ouch!" she cried "They might have grown a millimeter."

She noticed a letter opener sitting on the nightstand. With the pointed end of the blade, she pricked her index finger. A small drop of blood formed. Anna rubbed the bright-red blood on her lips to add color to them. Still nude, she pranced around in front of the mirror, pretending to be a model strutting on the runway. She began to fantasize that she was a famous movie actress attending a gala motion-picture premiere, being applauded by thousands of adoring fans. "*Xie xie*—thank you, thank you. To all the little people, I thank you," voiced Anna with mock appreciation.

A real clap of the hands startled her.

"Bravo! Bravo! Encore, encore!"

Anna pivoted to see the director's wife standing by the door, clapping her hands with gusto.

Deeply embarrassed, Anna tried to cover herself with her arms and hands.

Priscilla laughed uproariously. "Dear girl, I am a middle-aged woman. I have seen naked bodies, both male and female, on many occasions." She lifted the robe off the floor and placed it over Anna's shoulders. She then heartily hugged Anna, kissing her firmly on the lips.

"Welcome to my humble abode, Miss Anna May Wong. Dear girl, you need not be embarrassed by your play acting or your lack of clothing. I also pretend; pretend to be happy, pretend that my husband loves me... I could have been as great an actress as our dear friend Lilly," proclaimed Priscilla as she too began to strut about like a peacock.

Priscilla's breath reeked of whiskey.

"Mrs. Lawrence, I—"

"Please, call me Cilla. Or better yet, Mama Cilla."

Cilla walked to the bed and pulled out a bottle of whiskey she had hidden under the mattress. She shouted loudly for one of the maids. As commanded, the servant quickly entered the bedroom.

"Judy, bring us two shot glasses. My daughter and I will be having a wee drink to celebrate her debut," ordered Priscilla. "Oh, Judy, needless to say, we do not mention our little celebration to Mr. Lawrence."

The maid bowed obediently. "Yes, of course, Mrs. Lawrence."

As the maid left, Priscilla pulled back the front of Anna's robe. "Chelsea, you are so pencil thin, I must fatten you up."

"Mrs., uh, Mama Cilla, my name is Anna," Anna said politely.

Ignoring her correction, Priscilla closed Anna's robe and neatly tied the cloth waist belt.

"Chelsea, my own private stock, fifteen-year-old, single-barrel scotch, precisely the same age as you are, my daughter."

The maid returned with the glasses and Cilla quickly dismissed her with a wave of her hand.

Placing her arm over the girl's shoulder, Priscilla directed Anna out to the balcony. She motioned Anna to a chair and sat beside her.

As it was at Gish's mansion, the gardens were spectacular, with rolls of bright-red and yellow roses, manicured lawns, and ornate fountains.

After pulling the cork, Priscilla poured a good measure of the whiskey into the two shot glasses. She handed one to Anna. "To fame and fortune!"

Anna stared uncomfortably at the amber liquid in her glass. "Uh, Mama Cilla, I have never had strong drinks before."

Priscilla laughed. "Dear daughter, it's time you did. In any case, I do not like to drink alone. Now, drink," she commanded.

Anna remembered the countless times she had seen her father drunk, no doubt to momentarily escape his problems and his troubled life on the Gold Mountain.

She hesitantly put the glass to her lips and sipped. The liquid burned the length of her throat and she coughed. Priscilla slapped Anna's back.

"Daughter, it's like losing your virginity, it hurts the first time, then you get used to it, then eventually you love it, and finally, you can't live without it," giggled Priscilla. "The booze gets me through the day. Sharing a bed with your father no longer entertains me."

Though the taste of whiskey was an acquired one, and her first taste caused her to cough violently, Anna felt it empowering. As with most teenagers, wedged between the departure of childhood and the soon-to-be entrance into adulthood, she wanted to experiment with things that had been taboo to her.

She swallowed what remained of the liquor in her glass and again coughed and choked, but gradually Anna felt a sense of well-being, even more pleasing than the applause she'd received in her first acting role. "Cilla, more please."

"Daughter, that's *Mama* Cilla," corrected Priscilla, this time filling Anna's shot glass to the brim.

With the refill, Anna did not sip, but gulped the burning liquid as if it were weak tea.

"Chelsea, I've missed you so much..." Cilla slurred.

"I am not your daughter, Mrs. Lawrence," spoke Anna sharply, emboldened by the liquor.

With Priscilla's mind in a fog after years of consuming hard liquor, she did not hear Anna correcting her.

Realizing that Priscilla did not want to accept reality, Anna decided to be a part of the woman's fantasy for the time being. During the next hour, the two of them finished off the bottle of vintage whiskey.

"Chelsea, my daughter, I am on fire. Let us cool off in the pool."

Both inebriated, the two helped each other stand.

"Yes, Mama Cilla, I am on fire too. A swim would feel so good," voiced Anna in a slurred voice.

Staggering arm-in-arm, the two of them stood on shaky legs and walked to the staircase, where they lost their balance. The women rolled, arms and legs entwined, down the stairs and landed at the bottom with a loud crash. Their bodies, relaxed by the hard liquor, were not injured. Lying on their backs, Cilla and Anna laughed hysterically. Two servants rushed from the kitchen.

"Mrs. Lawrence, are you or Miss Wong hurt?" asked Judy.

Priscilla extended her hand. "Judy, give your mistress and her lovely daughter a hand up. Incidentally, would Chelsea or I be laughing like insane idiots if we were injured? Judy, my daughter and I will be going for a dip in the pool. Bring me a bath towel and the bottle of scotch I have hidden in the hallway planter."

The servant nodded her head in compliance "Oh, Mrs. Lawrence, do you wish for me to bring you and...uh...Miss Wong, uh, your daughter...two bathing suits?"

"Certainly not," responded Priscilla.

On wobbly legs, Priscilla and Anna held each other up as they walked outside to the Italian-marble pool. Priscilla kicked off her shoes and slowly pulled her dress straps off her shoulders, letting her dress fall in a heap at her bare feet. She then removed her undergarments. Once totally nude, Priscilla gently untied the bathrobe Anna was still wearing, allowing it to drop to her feet.

It was a peculiar site, two nude women facing each other for no particular reason other than the insanity of life in general. Judy the maid approached and placed the soft cotton bathrobe on the lawn chair and the fine scotch plus two glasses on the table. Judy, being a discreet and loyal servant, displayed no reaction to Mrs. Lawrence's eccentric behavior. She had witnessed similar behavior on many other occasions.

"Do you need anything else, Mrs. Lawrence?" asked the maid.

Priscilla said nothing in response.

The maid bowed politely, then left. Spontaneously, Priscilla swept Anna up in her arms and tossed her into the swimming pool.

Anna's head shot to the surface. Still giggling, she swam to the pool's edge.

"Chelsea, dear, how is the water?" asked Priscilla.

Anna held out her hand as if to indicate that she wanted a hand out of the water. Priscilla bent down and grabbed Anna's hand. With a hard tug, Anna pulled Priscilla into the pool.

"The water's fine, Mama," Anna giggled.

Like two silly school girlfriends, the two of them laughed while splashing water at each other. After diving under the water's surface, Anna playfully tickled Priscilla's feet, then shot back up to the surface. As her eyes began to focus, to her shock she saw Priscilla's husband, Chase, and her own mother, Lee You, standing at the pool's edge. A strong look of consternation was displayed on their faces as they watched Pricilla and Anna frolicking nude in the pool.

With numbing embarrassment, Priscilla was assisted out of the pool by her husband, while Anna's mother assisted her out of the pool.

Chase lifted the robe off the lawn chair, throwing it contemptuously at his wife while Lee You threw Anna's robe at her.

"Have you no shame, daughter? You shame me and your father. I no longer have a daughter!" exclaimed Lee You as she slapped Anna across the cheek.

Anna began to cry. "Forgive me, Mama. I guess I wanted to forget that I am just a lowly yellow girl my parents never wanted." She defiantly tossed her robe into the pool, then walked back inside the mansion, nude.

"Liu Tsong, I never want to see you again!" screamed Lee You as she observed the naked Anna stomping away.

Equally angry, Chase cursed, "Cilla, if you were not my wife I would report you to the authorities for being a child molester. Put some clothes on. I told the goddamn servants to report to me if you were hiding any booze around the house. I am firing the whole staff."

Priscilla dropped to her knees, grasping Chase's pants. "Please, don't blame the servants. I bribed them to buy me the bottles. They were only following my orders. You have your directing to keep you busy. Our daughter is dead. The bottle is my only escape from the loneliness."

Priscilla stood up and approached Anna's mother. "Mrs. Wong, I meant no harm to your daughter. She is the first person who has made me feel alive since my daughter died. I never touched your daughter. When I was a little girl, my own mama and I would swim naked in the creek behind our house. It was just harmless fun."

Lee You gazed at Priscilla with a confused look, uncertain whether to feel anger or pity for the woman. "Good day, Mrs. Lawrence," spoke Lee You glibly, then walked away.

"You disappoint me," said Lawrence, as he also departed to join Lee You.

Priscilla put on the robe and sat on the lawn chair, drinking from the second bottle of whiskey and brooding in the quiet solitude of the spacious garden grounds.

Likewise, Anna sat nude in the guest bedroom, brooding for hours. From her window, she could see the grand mansion called Pickfair in the distance. It was owned by celebrities Mary Pickford and her husband, Douglas Fairbanks. She watched the sunset as it gave Pickfair a dreamlike glow, making the structure look like a palace in a fairytale.

A soft knock on the door drew her attention, but Anna did not answer, not caring to see anyone. Slowly, the door opened.

"Oh, Anna, my apologies, I didn't know you were still undressed," voiced Lawrence, turning his back to her. "Anna dear, you have not eaten all day. Please dress and join Cilla and me for dinner. I have already spoken to Cilla. She has promised to behave herself. Please come to dinner. It's important you eat something to keep your strength up."

Anna pulled her dress over her head without bothering to put on her undergarments. "Mr. Lawrence, I will be down in a minute," responded Anna.

"Excellent! Cilla and I will see you shortly in the dining room."

Anna straightened out her dress. She paused for a moment to stare at Pickfair. "Someday you will be mine," mouthed Anna under her breath.

8

In bare feet, Anna walked to the head of the stairs. She straddled the banister, then, with a push, slid down it screaming at the top of her lungs like a madwoman. Rapidly gaining speed, her cries of glee quickly changed to cries of fear, thinking her joy ride might end in a dangerous crash.

In a blurred second, two strong arms snatched her from the railing before any possible injury could occur. "Miss Wong, you do enjoy a flashy entrance," quipped Lawrence as he held Anna in his arms.

"Sorry, Mr. Lawrence. My head is not on straight after having such an ugly day."

Lawrence gently placed Anna down on the floor. "Anna dear, call me Chase. It has indeed been a difficult day. Tomorrow will be a new, fresh day for all of us. Come, dine with Cilla and me." Lawrence led Anna by the hand into the dining room.

Priscilla was seated at one end of the long dining table. She was smoking a cigarette on a long silver stem, and grinned, nodding her head with uncomfortable courtesy.

A manservant pulled the chair out for Anna that was placed midway between Chase's and Priscilla's chairs. Another servant poured Anna hot tea into a porcelain teacup.

"The teapot, Anna, is a priceless object from the Ming Dynasty. Notice the new help? I fired Cilla's kiss-asses. The new help is a loan from your Auntie Lilly till I can find permanent domestics. But enough of this nonsense," voiced Lawrence as he snapped his fingers.

Yet another servant delivered some official-looking papers to Lawrence. With a pen made of pure gold he signed the document, then directed the servant to hand the papers to Anna.

"What is this?" she asked.

"Two documents, my precious child. The first document grants me temporary custody of you, and the second document is a contract with Summit Studios to act in six films. You'll be a corker, I promise you."

Lawrence stood and walked to Anna's chair, smiling enigmatically. He handed her the gold pen. "Sign the papers, my beautiful child, and you will have eternal life." Lawrence laughed hysterically. "Well, maybe not eternal life per se, but eternal life through your performances in my movies and those of other directors with almost as much talent as me."

Anna held the gold pen, staring blankly at the documents. She giggled. "I would rather have eternal life by not dying," she said as she signed both documents without reading a single word. "I suppose with my parents this is easier than drowning me," she added under her breath.

"What?" asked Lawrence.

"Nothing. My parents sold me. I guess drowning girl babies on the Gold Mountain is illegal," she joked bitterly.

Lawrence folded the documents and placed them in his inside breast pocket. "Keep the pen, my beloved protégé. Do not think harshly of your parents. They gave me verbal permission to be your guardian. They just need a little time apart from you, as you do from them, so everyone can clear their heads."

I have no mother, I have no father... thought Anna.

"My beloved child, you are welcome to stay with us as long as you have a mind to," spoke Lawrence as he kissed her on the cheek. Priscilla blew her a subtle kiss that Lawrence did not see.

In one short week, Anna went again before the camera. She was filming in Griffith Park, and once again played a lady of the evening.

Again the male lead was played by a white male made-up to look Asian. Anna worked six days a week, and Lawrence would place her in another film as quickly as the previous one was completed. Each time Anna portrayed a prostitute, or at least someone with a sordid past.

However, as Anna's career progressed her roles became more significant. She was earning five hundred dollars a week—a princely sum in the '20s. During her apprenticeship, she learned how to walk, talk, dress, and act like a glamorous actress. Young Anna May Wong had grown into a mature and attractive woman, but more importantly, she was learning the ins and outs of the movie-making business and how to become her own woman.

One day, Anna arrived home at the Lawrence mansion after another exhausting sixteen-hour day of shooting. The Lawrences' cook had prepared her a late-night dinner, a sparse meal composed of hot tea, yogurt, an orange, and a few grapes. Ravished, Anna inhaled the food. It was a sad scene—not unlike one of her movies—a young woman eating alone in a cavernous mansion's dining room.

"Anna, darling, you do not eat enough to satisfy a chipmunk," said Priscilla as she entered the dimly lit room.

Anna shrugged her shoulders, smiling with wry reflection. "Cilla, one of the drawbacks to being a flicker actress is my fans do not pay their fifteen cents to watch a fat Anna May Wong on the Silver Screen. Where have you been, my friend? I've not seen you in over a month."

Priscilla wiped away a tear that trickled down her cheek. "My bastard husband forbade me to associate with you. Me being an insane woman, he thought I might corrupt you. Chase is grooming you to become a major star. God forbid I might screw it up." Priscilla leaned down and kissed Anna on the cheek. "But my workaholic husband is working late reviewing the day's shooting, so I came to see you. I've missed you so much, my daughter."

Anna shoved the food off the table, sending the plates crashing onto the red marble floor. "Damn it, Cilla, I am *not* your daughter. I have no mother."

"Anna, my love, you could be. Please do not turn your back on me." Priscilla rang the servant's bell, and a young black girl rushed into the kitchen. "Georgia, bring me the bottle I have hidden in the hat box in the guest bedroom."

"Certainly," responded the obedient maid, bowing politely before leaving. With haste, the maid returned with the whiskey bottle.

"Georgia, leave," commanded Priscilla, giggling with a silly arrogance. "My foolish husband thought that a new staff would not keep secret my hiding places for my booze. Silly man. Slip enough money under the table and the domestic help would kill for me. Even during Prohibition in America, a person can buy good booze for medicinal purposes." Priscilla tossed the tea onto the floor, then poured the expensive whiskey into Anna's teacup.

Anna hadn't had strong liquor since the day she and Priscilla were caught swimming nude in the pool. She remembered the warm feeling of euphoria she felt and the terrible hangover she had the following day. But, she was convinced that the rewards outweighed the consequences and drank the contents of the cup with a single, quick gulp. The second time around, the whiskey didn't burn as much going down and she didn't cough. Anna pointed her index finger at the cup, indicating a refill. Priscilla filled the cup and again Anna consumed the full measure in a quick gulp.

Priscilla pulled up a chair beside Anna, and kissed her on the lips. "You don't leave me, Anna. There is no one else that I feel so much compassion for. Can you at least pretend to love me?"

Emboldened by the strong drink, Anna replied, "Mrs. Lawrence, I will never be your daughter. You are a drunk, empty, gwah lo woman with an empty soul."

Priscilla stood up, glaring at Anna contemptuously. Drinking directly from the bottle, she swiftly consumed almost all of what remained in it. She then violently threw the whiskey bottle at the ornate mirror that hung above the fireplace mantle. The loud sound of shattering glass brought several of the servants rushing into the dining room.

"Get the hell out of here!" Priscilla barked at them. "I have not yet finished my conversation with Miss Wong."

Shocked by their mistresses' odd behavior, the servants left the room as ordered.

As usual, Priscilla was intoxicated. "Don't you dare look down on me just because you have a few small roles under your belt. Hear this, my yellow whore. I was once a great actress in my own right, then I fell in love with a son-of-a-bitch named Chase Lawrence—or at least, I *thought* it was love. I fell for his bullshit that to be a whole woman I must be a dutiful wife and mother. Then, when Chelsea was born dead, I became an insignificant zero to my husband. When I wanted to return to acting, he said I had lost my edge; that the fire in my belly had died along with Chelsea. What little affection Chase might have had for me evaporated like dew on a hot summer day when the doctors informed us that because of some kind of disease, I cannot bear more children. Chase finds his pleasure with the nubile starlets that would do anything to obtain a role in one of his films. Why did my dear husband not try to bed you as well, you wonder? He has said you are the daughter he always wanted."

Priscilla laughed while lighting herself a cigarette.

"No doubt my husband, who has a heart of stone, was impressed by your balls. You're the only pubescent girl who didn't try to get in his pants to try to get acting work."

Anna snatched the cigarette from Priscilla's hand and took a long drag. "Cilla, these things are so relaxing. I had my first taste of tobacco a few months ago when I was required to smoke cigarettes in Lon Chaney's *Bits of Life*. I played his wife. It was the first time I didn't play a whore and was my first screen credit." She gazed out the window at the bright full moon as she reflected. She giggled. "I was quite proud of that role."

Priscilla began to laugh, seemingly amused by Anna's statement. "Dear girl, your tiny role in Chaney's movie was only an appetizer.

The main course of lobster, rare filet mignon, and other delicacies can be yours. All you have to do is ask."

Pricilla kissed her. Unlike the previous occasion when she had kissed Anna as a mother would give her child a tender peck, this kiss was more like a gangster planting the kiss of death upon a victim.

Anna was quite perplexed by the woman's curious statement. "Cilla, what the hell are you telling me?"

Priscilla retrieved her cigarette from Anna and took a drag. "Anna, the love of my life, have you ever heard of the actor Douglas Fairbanks?"

"Don't be silly. Of course I have. Fairbanks is a big star. He, in fact, lives across the street with his equally big star wife, Mary Pickford. What of it?"

Priscilla playfully blew a ring of smoke in Anna's face. "Doug saw you in *The Toll of the Sea*. He was quite taken by your performance. He wants you to appear in his next swashbuckler movie, *The Thief of Baghdad*. Doug will give you top billing...below him, of course."

Quite startled by the revelation, Anna sat down. "Why didn't Chase tell me about Fairbanks wanting me to be in his movie?"

Priscilla sat back down beside Anna. She put a comforting hand on Anna's knee.

"Dear girl, Doug and Mary own their own studio, Universal. Have you forgotten, young lady, that you sold your soul to Chase and Summit Studio? The contract you signed with Summit is chiseled in granite. My son-of-a-bitch husband and Summit will never release you. And what a pity. Doug's film would make you the only Chinese-American featured actor in America."

"Cilla, I want this goddamn role. I *need* this role. Please talk to Chase for me."

Priscilla chuckled. "Young lady, do you mean you are tired of playing whores in almost every 'flicker' you appear in? Anna May Wong is the only Chinese actress's name I see on any screen credits."

Anna shook her head. "It's not enough. Gwah los stop me on the street and ask me for my autograph, but I am not sure what they are looking at. Am I a respected actress they admire or am I the Siamese twins, two brothers stuck together that people paid a nickel to gawk at?"

"Perhaps a little of both. You want me to convince Chase to loan you out to Doug so bleached-skin people such as I will no longer see a chink? I would be delighted to paint you white, for a price."

Anna sighed with exasperation. "Cilla, you know how much I want this role. What do you want in return?"

Priscilla leaned toward her and began rubbing Anna's breasts. "I told you, Anna dear, how lonely I became after Chelsea died. The bottle is a poor substitute for companionship. I asked you to be my daughter and you ignored me. You will not ignore me anymore—that is, if you want me to speak to Chase about getting you that meaty role you are so hungry for."

Anna contemplated Priscilla's proposal. She embraced Priscilla. "Cilla...Mama...please help me. I will do whatever you ask of me."

Priscilla grinned, pressing her fingers against her lips, then placing her fingers against Anna's lips. "My dearest daughter, tomorrow is a rare day off for you. We can sleep in."

As ordered by Priscilla, Anna would share a bed with her. Anna undressed and slipped nervously into bed with Priscilla, who cradled her as if she were a small child. The older woman's advances were not of a sexual nature, but were certainly abnormal. Nonetheless, Anna played along with Priscilla's eccentricities for the sake of her career advancement.

While she rested her head on Priscilla's breasts, Anna reflected on the rare moments when her own mother, Lee You, would hold her when she was a little girl and was frightened by a stormy night, or had a scraped knee, but gradually, Lee You grew distant from her. Anna was not sure why her mother had stopped loving her. Perhaps Lee You had her own demons to battle and forgot she had a daughter who also had dragons to slay.

Given the awkwardness of the situation, Anna found it hard to sleep. Lying in the coal-black night, she could hear the soft sounds of the water that flowed in the marble fountain just outside the bedroom window in the garden. She began to feel pity for Priscilla in place of annoyance. She covered her mouth to muffle a sudden burst of laughter.

No doubt, I too will be a crazy woman when I reach middle-age, she thought.

After finally falling asleep, she was awakened by the aroma of strong coffee. "Chelsea, darling, it's almost ten. You're sleeping your life away."

Anna rubbed the sleep from her eyes to see a smiling Priscilla holding a cup of steaming coffee near her nose. By her side on the bed sat a breakfast tray of ham and eggs and a fresh red rose. Though Anna preferred the taste of hot tea, she drank the coffee willingly to please Priscilla and to clear the fog from her half-asleep mind. Priscilla placed the breakfast tray on Anna's lap. As she munched heartily on jellied toast, a small glob of blackberry jelly fell on her bare left breast. Though not totally at ease with the delusional woman, Anna had no qualms about being nude in front of Priscilla. After all, they had partied together and had frolicked naked in the pool.

Inexplicitly, Pricilla lowered her head to lick the blackberry jelly that had landed precisely on Anna's hardened nipple. Disturbed by Priscilla's quirky act, Anna threw the breakfast tray onto the floor, then harshly pushed Priscilla off the bed. "Don't touch me like that. I am not your girl toy," spat Anna.

Priscilla broke down and began to sob heavily. "Please forgive me, Chelsea—I mean, Anna. I meant no harm. I am just a silly, desperate, lonely, middle-aged housewife that no one in this whole world gives a shit about, or cares whether I live or die. Please forgive me," she begged, her face buried in her hands.

Anna rose from the bed. She lifted Priscilla up to embrace her. "Crazy gwah lo bitch. I thought only chinks and other children of inferior colors knew loneliness and rejection. We're two bitches with little value." Anna undid the woman's negligee and kissed Priscilla on her left breast. "Mama, did you know one term the Chinese have for whites is lo fon? It loosely translates as 'old rice.' In other words, you whites have as much value to us Chinese as old rice."

Priscilla laughed as Anna wiped away her tears. "Well, I certainly didn't think lo fon meant 'white people we know and love.'"

The two women began to laugh hysterically.

"Incidentally, Mama dearest, gwah lo is even more derogatory. It loosely translates as 'white devil.'"

With a better understanding of each other, the two women dressed. Pricilla ordered the chauffeur to drive the car around to the front of the house, and the jovial pair embarked on a shopping trip.

9

A nna's mother had never taken her shopping for new clothes. She had always worn hand-me-downs from relatives and clothing donated by customers whose children had outgrown them. Anna felt elated as she and Priscilla entered a high-end clothing store.

"Welcome, Mrs. Lawrence!" gushed the store manager. "We've not seen you in ages. Your assistant is also most welcome."

Priscilla giggled. "Winston, this young lady is not my assistant, maid, cook, or a lackey. Miss Wong is my a dear friend, and in fact, she is like my own daughter."

The manager flashed a forced smile. "Uh, Mrs. Lawrence, you have been a loyal customer for years. You are welcome at our store always; however, the young lady is new to this establishment. We prefer patrons we are familiar with. May we recommend that Miss Wong patronize Woolworth's Five and Dime? I feel confident she will find something suitable there," the man said with pretentious sincerity.

Priscilla sneered at the manager contemptuously. "Winston, you always were a horse's ass. Spare me the phony courtesies. Why not tell me in a language both Anna and I can understand? Your store does not allow chinks to shop here."

The manager, as well as the employees and the other a patrons, were shocked by Priscilla's brash outspokenness.

Too embarrassed to look at Priscilla directly, the manager looked coyly at the floor. "Mrs. Lawrence, I am deeply sorry if you took offense at my suggestion. I am only following the rules set by the administrators. Rules are rules. If your Chinese acquaintance objects to it, she can go back to China to shop."

Anna displayed no reaction as she felt the texture of a bright-red evening dress that adorned a mannequin. "What a pretty dress. I do not think I would find such a fine dress in China. Sir, I wish to buy this one," stated Anna.

The manager shook his head, quite exasperated. "Young lady, I am only following store policy. As I have already explained to Mrs. Lawrence, I cannot sell the dress to you."

Reacting quickly, Priscilla said, "Winston, I will purchase the red dress. Put it on my account." She giggled nervously.

The manager bowed politely. "Very well, Mrs. Lawrence. Sara, please box the red dress for Mrs. Lawrence," he said to a store clerk.

Anna slapped the clerk's hand as she attempted to remove the dress from the mannequin. "No, Mother, I will buy the dress. I am Chinese. We yellows consider red good luck. It would be bad luck to gift me a red dress when purchased from a gwah lo named Winston. It is only good luck if I purchase the dress with my own money," stated Anna with biting sarcasm.

Winston rolled his eyes as his temper and patience grew increasingly short. "Miss Wong, do not get snippy with me. I explained to you most politely that I cannot sell you the dress. I kindly compromised by allowing Mrs. Lawrence to purchase the dress for you. Young woman, leave the premises now or I will be forced to call the authorities and have you arrested for trespassing."

Priscilla took Anna by the arm. "My daughter, there are many other clothing stores in Beverly Hills. We don't need these cheap rags."

Anna pulled her arm away from Priscilla and sat on the floor. True to the manager's threat, the police soon arrived. After a brief conversation with the manager, the police approached Anna, who remained sitting statue-like on the floor.

The lead police officer said, "Anna May Wong, I have been told by your friend Mrs. Lawrence that you are some kinda movie actress and you are to be treated with serious respect. I used to work in Chinatown. You Chinks usually know better than to make waves. I don't care if you are some movie star. If you don't get off your ass now and walk outta this store that caters to decent Christian white people, I will throw your ass in the can for trespassing and disturbing the peace."

Priscilla bent down to whisper in Anna's ear. "Anna, my daughter, I beg you. Please walk out of the store with me this instant. You have your reputation as a highly regarded actress to consider. Any whiff of scandal could damage your career. You also need to think of the Chinese youth who look up to you."

Anna flashed a forced grin. "Cilla, let my yellow brothers and sisters earn their own self-respect. I cannot help my fellow Chinese or lift them up by playing a whore in a dozen movies." With that said, Anna spat defiantly on the lead policeman's nicely polished shoes.

"Yellow bitch!" sneered the policeman as he savagely struck Anna across her back with his baton.

Anna cried out in pain as he and his partner struck her again and again on her head, arms, and torso.

"Stop it! Stop it! You bastards, you're killing Anna!" shouted Priscilla.

The store manager and a store clerk forcefully held Priscilla to prevent her from being injured as well.

Blood flowed down Anna's forehead. Though in unbearable pain, Anna continued to sit on the floor, stubbornly refusing to budge. She soon lost consciousness and the two police officers lifted her off the floor.

"Open the goddamn door," ordered one of the officers to a salesclerk as he and his partner carried the severely beaten Anna to the squad vehicle.

As they reached the street, a group of teenaged Chinese schoolgirls exiting a school bus recognized Anna as the officers were placing her in the back seat of their car.

"Ah! It's Anna May Wong, the Chinese movie star!" screeched one schoolgirl.

"What happened?" cried another.

"The son-of-a-bitch city police beat Miss Wong for trying to purchase a red dress," announced Priscilla.

Enraged by the police's brutality toward their screen idol, the schoolgirls began cursing, assaulting the officers with their schoolbooks, and kicking them in the shins.

The situation had turned into a maddening melee.

"Damn little chink girls, get the hell outta here before we arrest the whole lot of yah!" shouted one officer as he and his partner struggled to position the unconscious Anna inside the police car.

Finally, after a great deal of pushing and shoving, the officers managed to speed away, the frenzied Chinese girls cursing until the squad vehicle was no longer in sight.

Upon arriving at the police station, the arresting officers carried Anna into an empty cell and dropped her limp body onto a cot as if she were a sack of potatoes. The lead officer spat on the still unconscious woman.

"Have a good night's sleep, chink," voiced the officer.

Though severely beaten, Anna's senses were still intact. Her soul hovered over her motionless body. She heard the Chinese girls protesting her arrest and sensed the policeman who had spat on her after being dropped abruptly onto the cot. She visualized entering a room with brilliant, blinding lights. A gold statue sat on a table. She felt invisible hands pulling her away as she came within a fraction of an inch of grabbing the statue. Then she saw the faint image of a gwah lo woman dressed as a Chinese peasant snatching the statue.

Anna began to hear a distant voice calling her name. She was gradually returning to consciousness. She opened her eyes. As they focused, she saw several people standing over her—the concerned faces of her parents, Chase, Priscilla, a physician, and several nurses. With Lawrence's influence, he had Anna transferred from jail to a nearby hospital.

Lee You tenderly kissed Anna's right hand as Priscilla kissed her left hand, the two women on either side of Anna's hospital bed.

"Father, Mother...long time no see," spoke Anna in a soft, labored voice.

Lee You lifted Anna's hand again to kiss the back of it. "My precious daughter, when they told your father and I what had happened, we were so afraid that we had lost you. Please don't leave. We have so much time to make-up for," said Lee You, crying.

Father Sam Sing crowded in beside Lee You at Anna's bedside. Like most Chinese men, he was too proud to show emotion and his facial expression remained stoic. His eyes narrowed as he fought back his emotions. "Liu Tsong...or Anna May if that is what you want to be called...I want you to know that your mother and I went to the theater to watch you in *Toll of the Sea*. It was the first color flicker I ever saw. Your acting was not bad. Being parents of the movie star Anna May Wong, the usher even let us sit in the middle row. When I heard what happened to you, I wanted to buy a gun and kill those gwah lo bastard policemen who hurt my daughter, but your guardian Mr. Lawrence reminded me they are gwah los and gwah lo laws protect thcm. Mr. Lawrence is a rich and powerful movie director. He has assured me he will avenge the terrible pain they have caused you."

Sam Sing fought to express words he had never said to Anna her entire life. "Anna May Wong, you are my daughter, flesh of my flesh blood of my blood. I was never much of a father to you. I am so sorry. I beg your forgiveness." Sam Sing was no longer able to contain his emotions and cried.

Anna looked at her father, seeing a different kind of man than she was accustomed to. "Sam Sing, you are right. You were never much of a father, but it is not easy being a Chinese man, and it is not easy being a Chinese woman. It may be too late for the two of us to have a relationship. I need to climb the Gold Mountain and may not have time for a mother and father who should have been there to battle my demons when I was a little girl, afraid of the dark. I will need time to think about what we are to each other. Father, Mother, let me heal and we will have a long conversation about this later."

Jealous of the possible new bond Anna might make with her parents, and being protective, Priscilla snapped, "Anna needs her rest. She is seriously injured. Please leave now. I will contact you when your daughter is well enough to receive visitors."

Anna reached out to hold Priscilla's hand. "Yes, Cilla...Mama Cilla...I am very tired...no more visitors."

Shocked by their daughter's cold dismissal, Lee You broke down in tears. She leaned toward Anna to kiss her in farewell. Anna turned her head away so that the kiss would land on her cheek rather than her lips.

Sam Sing bowed politely. "Take care, Anna. Yes, please let us have that conversation. I want to get to know my daughter, and I want her to know her father." He blew her a parting kiss.

Anna received more than a dozen stitches to her head, had broken ribs, and numerous bruises across most of her body. She was hospitalized for two weeks. Each day she was visited by Priscilla, who had forbidden Anna's parents to visit. She lied to Anna, telling her that her parents were ignoring her.

Every day Priscilla would bring her scripts with roles she felt Anna would be suited for. She read to Anna classic stories by Charles Dickens and the Bronte sisters. When Anna was feeling better, Priscilla brought Anna's beloved Chinese pastries, dim sum. Anna was beginning to feel as close a bond with Priscilla as she had had with Lillian.

But as close as Anna was feeling toward Priscilla, she would not give herself totally as she had done with Lillian. All her life she had been told by family members to distrust the gwah los. It was difficult to give her soul to anyone, of any color, as would most people who had been shunned and ridiculed in their childhood.

When the day came at last for Anna to be released from the hospital, Priscilla came for her in a chauffeur-driven Duesenberg. As they rode together, Priscilla was uncharacteristically solemn and preoccupied with something.

Wanting to break the tension, Anna smiled. "Cilla, isn't it so crazy that I am now a recorded criminal? Whoever heard of someone being charged for wanting to buy a red dress," she giggled.

Priscilla grinned slightly and placed a hand on Anna's knee. "Daughter, don't be concerned about such nonsense. The Summit Studios lawyers are the best in California. They easily got the authorities to drop all charges against you."

"And what of Mr. Fairbanks's movie that he wants me to appear in? In a week or two I will be good as new."

Priscilla seemed quite uncomfortable at hearing Anna's question. "Honey, you need to talk to Chase. I have already told my husband about your desire to act in Doug's film. It would be best that he discusses the matter with you than you learn secondhand from me."

Anna felt deep apprehension after hearing Priscilla's response. She knew from Priscilla's lack of enthusiasm that Chase's response to her request would only be negative.

As they pulled up to the grand Lawrence mansion, Anna was very surprised to see the façade decorated with brightly colored ribbons, balloons, and an enormous banner with the words "Welcome home, Anna" written on it. The mansion's dozen servants lined the steps leading to the front entrance. Chase stood at the top of the steps, applauding along with the servants to welcome her home.

With open arms, Chase embraced Anna, kissing her on the lips in a more-than-friendly manner. Though she was quite ambulatory, Chase and her doctors insisted she be transported in a wheelchair.

Two athletic black servants carried Anna in her wheelchair up the steps, then wheeled her into the house. Escorted by Chase, Priscilla, and the servants, she was rolled into the mansion's ballroom. A huge, six-layer cake sat in the middle of the twenty-foot-long mahogany dining table. Anna was equally surprised to see Lillian Gish, Douglas Fairbanks, and his wife Mary Pickford as they rushed forward to welcome her. A black man dressed in a tuxedo began to play a Ragtime tune on a grand piano.

Anna stood up to embrace Gish. "Auntie Lilly! What a surprise. I missed you so much. Forgive me. I was mad at you because you went behind my back to get me my first acting job. I wanted to make it on my own, but you were only looking out for me, to help me stand on my own two feet. I was too proud to have a redheaded gwah lo pull me up."

"For goodness sakes, child, Chinese girls do not have a monopoly on pig-headedness. Allow me to introduce you to my sister, Dorothy, someday. And your own Auntie Lilly has been deemed by some to be a stubborn bitch." Gish laughed uproariously. "What is most important is that you recover from your terrible horse riding accident. Do not forget I am your Auntie Lilly. I love you like my own daughter. Come back to my home to recuperate if you wish."

Anna was shocked that Gish thought she had been injured in a riding accident, but did not correct her. "Auntie, I almost forgot how kind you have been to me, but I have already promised to mend in the Lawrence house."

"Very well, but remember, dear, that my door will always be open to you. Incidentally, congratulations on your upcoming role in Doug's film. With you in it, it will certainly be a doozy." She smiled warmly. "Take care, my love."

Fairbanks was standing nearby, anxious to speak to Anna.

"Anna May Wong, we meet at last. I am so sorry to hear about your riding accident. Please allow me to introduce myself. I'm Douglas Fairbanks, and this little pixie of a girl standing beside me is my talented wife Mary Pickford."

Anna's heart began to pound loudly as her pulse raced. She was overcome with emotion at meeting two of the most popular and powerful actors in the motion-picture industry.

"I-I...Mr. Fairbanks, Miss Pickford, I am so honored to be standing in the presence of two of the world's greatest actors," stammered Anna in a quivering voice.

The couple chuckled with amusement.

Pickford playfully slapped Anna's hand. "Miss Wong, you have been reading too many of those Hollywood gossip papers. Did you also read that Doug and I are up for sainthood?" joked Pickford.

Anna giggled. "Mr. Fairbanks, I am so grateful you have chosen me to be in your next flicker. It will be a doozy," added Anna, mimicking Gish's slang.

Fairbanks and Pickford flashed an astonished gaze at Anna.

"But, but Miss Wong, Chase informed us some time ago that you were not interested in appearing in *The Thief of Baghdad*...that your loyalty to him is too strong to act for anyone else," stated a confused Fairbanks.

"Chase Lawrence is a lying gwah lo son-of-a-bitch!" cried Anna, and stormed away to find Chase.

"Anna, darling, you appear to have made a rapid recovery," Chase said sarcastically, impressed by her quick steps toward him.

"Lying gwah lo bastard!" shouted Anna as she slapped the champagne glass from Chase's hand.

"Miss Wong, let us not make an embarrassing scene in front of everyone. Follow me. Any grievance you have, you can tell me in private."

Anna followed Chase to his study. He politely held the door open for her as she stomped into the room. The instant Chase closed the door behind them, Anna slapped his face.

"My, aren't you a saucy tempered little girl," spoke Chase, rubbing his cheek. "So, what is troubling my little protégé?"

"You lied to Doug Fairbanks and Auntie Lilly that I was injured riding a horse. I have never been on a horse in my life. You also fed horse shit to Fairbanks that I was not interested in acting in his next movie project."

Chase poured himself a glass of brandy, then settled down on a leather couch. He took several sips of the brandy, avoiding eye contact with Anna. After a bit of contemplation, he gazed at her. "My beautiful, talented girl. Everything I do or say is with your welfare in mind. Of course, I made up the story about how you received your injuries. The tabloid papers would eat you for breakfast if they knew the truth, and they would twist the truth by saying you instigated your battle with the cops in a drunken rage."

"You told my parents that you would make the police pay for nearly beating me to death. Was that also a lie?"

Chase chuckled with biting coldness. "Anna, wake up and join the real world. Unlike in the movies, the good guys do not always win. In fact, the good guys and women usually lose, regardless of what some people might think. I am not God. The cops said you attacked them, that they were only defending themselves. Just your word against theirs. I went to the studio head. The bastard laughed in my face when I asked about suing the police department. If you were a white woman star like Mary Pickford or Gloria Swanson, my studio would defend you to no end. But alas, Anna, you are only a lowly Chinese girl."

"And what am I to you?"

Chase placed his hand under her chin, lifting her head so that the two would look each other in the eyes. "China girl, it was Cilla's idea for me to be your mentor. Before Chelsea was stillborn, we spoke of grooming our future daughter or son to be a major film star. The wife saw you once, sitting on a Buddha statue in Chinatown, sneaking a peek at one of the many films I shot. Cilla was visiting the set in one of her usual drunken binges to inform me that she was leaving me for the hundredth time. Then she saw the cute little China girl and told me in her usual ridiculous logic that to have a China girl daughter to care for would heal our stormy relationship." Chase took another long swallow of brandy. "And that, dear girl, is recent history in a nutshell. You signed a piece of paper and now you are the property of Mr. and Mrs. Chase Lawrence."

Anna snatched the glass from Chase and gulped what remained of the brandy. "Mr. Lawrence, because I am your property you lied to Mr. Fairbanks that I did not want to be in his movie...out of fear of losing your hold on me?"

Chase showed Anna a devil-like grin, "My, my. For a naïve

China girl, you catch on fast. You still have one or two days of shooting in order to complete our current film. This marks the sixth movie you have acted in for Summit Studios. If you recall, the contract was for you to appear in six films for Summit; however, had you read the fine print, you would have noticed that Summit holds the option to have you solely act in Summit films in perpetuity."

"Perpetuity?" asked a confused Anna.

"Dear girl, that's fancy gwah lo talk. *Perpetuity* means forever and a day. Well, forever, anyway. 'And a day' was only a bit of my humor. Remember when you camped out at the entrance to Summit Studios looking to me for salvation? If you had not come, I would have tracked you down in any case."

Anna poured herself another measure of brandy and swallowed it in one swift gulp. "Mr. Lawrence..."

"Call me Chase."

"Mr. Lawrence," repeated Anna. "Am I to understand that you will not allow me to appear in the Fairbanks film, or any other movie that does not have the Summit stamp on it?"

Lawrence glared at her with a rather demonic grin. "Anna May Wong, I could have a word with my boss. He is a reasonable man. He would probably loan you out to Doug or anyone else, but I want to know how much of your soul you want to sell to the devil to become the world's first Asian woman movie star."

With those words, Lawrence began to unbutton Anna's blouse. Anna pushed his hands away.

"Mr. Lawrence, when we first met I asked you if you wanted to bed me in exchange for a role in one of your flickers. You didn't seem interested. What changed your mind?"

Lawrence kissed Anna amorously on her lips. "Dear lady, when we first met you were a hairless child of only fourteen. There is now a bit more fuzz on the peach. You're now a grown woman of twenty-one. Now give me that goddamn pound of flesh and you will become a shining star," exclaimed Lawrence.

Anna began to shiver. She sat on a chair, drinking more brandy directly from the bottle and weighing her options. She repeatedly played Lawrence's words over in her mind. She began to cry with deep humiliation and guilt. She stood up and slowly completed the undressing that Lawrence had begun, then stood naked, with the exception of her heavily bandaged ribs, before Lawrence.

"Mr. Lawrence, you win. I am selling my soul to become a famous actress. It means more to me than my life."

Lawrence refilled his glass with brandy. He circled around her, her eyeing her like a rancher examining a champion bull.

"Damn you, Mr. Lawrence, get it over with. You wanted me, so take me!" cried Anna impatiently.

Lawrence began to laugh hysterically. He lifted her chin with his finger and kissed Anna gently on the lips.

"Silly, silly, Chinese girl. I have pussy that falls off trees for me. I was only testing you to see how much you really wanted it. I don't want your body. I've decided to steal your soul instead. Get dressed. Let's rejoin the party in your honor."

Feeling guilt and humiliation, Anna put on her clothes and walked to the door. Lawrence held the door open for her.

"Incidentally, my protégé, I am not allowing you to appear in Doug's film, or any other film not owned by Summit. Let *me* make you a star."

Anna couldn't believe her ears. Clutching her painful ribs, she ran past the startled guests and out into the garden.

10

Anna rested beside one of the numerous marble fountains on the mansion grounds. She placed her head under the water that flowed from the pitcher held by a marble statue of a nude wood nymph. The cool water soothed her troubled soul.

Feeling invigorated, Anna grabbed one of the large rocks that encircled a rose bed. Deeply angered and frustrated, she whacked the arm of the finely carved statue, breaking it. Anna then vented her anger on the carved marble pitcher. After much pounding, the marble pitcher shattered and water shot out forcefully. Abruptly, the offending rock was snatched from Anna's hands. She pivoted to see Gish standing behind her.

"Anna my sweet, you think you can erase your troubles by damaging a priceless Italian-marble sculpture?" quipped Gish as she returned the rock to the rose bed.

Anna burst into tears. Gish, in turn, wrapped her arms around Anna.

"Tell Auntie Lilly what is troubling you, my child."

"Auntie Lilly, you already know that Douglas Fairbanks wants me to appear in his next movie."

"Yes, that film will put you one step closer to being a star," stated Gish.

"The bastard Lawrence will not allow me to appear in the Fairbanks movie, or any other movie not owned by Summit Studios. The contract I signed forces me to only act in Summit films in perpetuity. That means—"

"Yes, dear girl, I know what *perpetuity* means. Those son-of-a-bitch studio moguls also tried to enslave me forever. Because I was an inexperienced teenage girl standing a mere five feet tall, they didn't think I had the testicles to fight back. With my sister Dorothy at my side, I fought those bastards and became one of the first actresses to form my own production company. I am now free to do as I damn well please. Let me think about your situation. You have two more days of filming in our current movie with Chase. I will have a word with Doug and my lawyers and get back to you in a few days. The devil did not buy your soul, my child. You only pawned it. I'll just have to find a way to buy you back."

Anna kissed Gish on the cheek. "Thank you, Auntie Lilly. Please do all you can to pull me out of purgatory."

The following morning, Anna returned to the movie set. She fought through the pain of her broken ribs to begin the final two days of filming. Clearly, there was friction between her and Lawrence.

"God damn it, girl, let me see emotion! You're supposed to display joy in this scene, but you act more like you're constipated."

Anna grimaced. "Mr. Lawrence, my ribs have not yet healed. I am in much pain."

The director became even more outraged by Anna's excuse. "Miss Wong, I don't care if you're having a heart attack. Need I remind you, this is a silent movie! The audience cannot hear the reflection in your voice. All you have to show them is the expression on that pretty face of yours. I want to remind you that you have signed an iron-clad contract with Summit Studios. There's nothing on that piece of paper that says we have to pay you to act. I could assign you to cleaning the shit houses. Come to think of it, that's probably all you slants are good for. So, start pretending you are overjoyed at the birth of your illegitimate child. It's called *acting.* So act, or you will have to trim your long, green fingernails so you can clean the shitters!" screamed Lawrence at the top of his lungs in front of the entire film crew.

Anna's temper began to boil but she did as she was told. She knew Lawrence's harsh scolding was only to show his power over her and all the other actors. Fighting through her physical discomfort and Lawrence's constant bullying, Anna completed the final two days of filming.

"A very sorry piece of acting, Miss Wong. Let's hope that in our next movie you show a little more personality than a rock," stated Lawrence as he tossed her the script for their next film.

Later, Anna was lying on the sofa in her dressing room, exhausted from the sixteen-hour film shoot. Lawrence stopped by to be sure she had reviewed the new script. An assistant placed a damp face towel on her forehead. Without even looking at the script, Anna tossed it in the trash can.

"Bitch! Pick it up!" commanded Lawrence.

"Missy Wong, I'll get the script for you," spoke the loyal female assistant, pulling it from the trash.

Forcefully, Lawrence snatched the script out of the assistant's hand. "No! I want Miss Wong to pick it up," he stated, tossing it back into the trash can.

Anna and Lawrence's eyes locked. They glared at each other contemptuously.

"Miss Wong, we begin filming our next movie in a few days. You damn well had better be ready. Read the script now, or I'll have you eating it."

Anna closed her eyes tightly and dabbed her face with the damp face towel. "Mr. Lawrence, a couple of gwah lo policemen beat me till I almost died. I have not yet recovered fully and yet you want me to begin acting in another flicker after only five days of rest?"

Lawrence savagely yanked Anna off the sofa and shook her fiercely, exacerbating the pain from her injuries.

"Anna I've told you a thousand times, call me Chase! And hear this, my yellow bitch. You are my property! I created you! You do exactly what I tell you or I will destroy you."

Defiantly, Anna spat in Lawrence's face. In turn, Lawrence slapped Anna. Dazed, Anna began to fall, but Lawrence held her up. He made a fist and was about to strike her again, but a knock on the dressing room door interrupted the assault.

"Who the hell is it?" shouted Lawrence.

"The Grim Reaper, you son-of-a-bitch," responded a feminine voice from the other side of the door.

Lawrence knew immediately that the woman behind the voice was Gish. Without permission to enter, Lillian Gish, Douglas Fairbanks, and Gish's attorney barged into the tiny dressing room.

"Lilly, Doug! What a delightful surprise," said Lawrence. "What brings the two of you here at this hour of the night?"

Anna ran to Gish's side and clutched her hands.

"Chase, you always were an arrogant horse's ass. Anna is going home with me and she is going to act in Doug's next movie, and any goddamn movie she wishes as long as it's not owned by Summit," shrieked Gish.

"Ah! Excuse me, Miss Gish! The all-seeing, all-knowing goddess movie star has ordained that Miss Anna May Wong is no longer affiliated with Summit Studios and their humble servant Chase Lawrence," spoke Lawrence, bowing in sarcastic retort. He began to chuckle. "Must I remind you, Lilly and Doug, that Miss Wong signed a very legal contract that binds her to Summit until hell freezes over."

"Not quite, dear boy," quipped Fairbanks as he forcefully shoved Chase onto a chair. "It is better you hear this sitting down. This fine-looking gentleman that came with Miss Gish and me is Mr. Jonathan Smithhart. He represents both Lilly and Mary, and my interests. Jonathan, explain the situation to Mr. Lawrence."

Smithhart came forward, pulling a document out of his attaché case. "Mr. Lawrence, I have in my hands a copy of the contract you had Miss Wong sign, binding her in perpetuity with Summit Studios."

"You idiot two-dollar, mail-order attorney! That contract is perfectly legal. That is Miss Wong's signature. She signed it of her own free will." Lawrence pointed to Anna's signature on the contract.

Gish, Fairbanks, and Smithhart laughed collectively.

"One minor detail, Mr. Lawrence," the attorney said. "Miss Wong was underage when she signed this contract. The law states no one under the age of eighteen can legally sign a document of any kind without the consent and cosigning of a parent or guardian. Mr. Lawrence, you should have had one of Miss Wong's parents cosign the document."

"You should consider yourself lucky that Anna's parents don't sue your ass," warned Fairbanks.

"Good day, Chase," spoke Gish as they turned to depart with Anna in tow.

"One moment, Auntie," spoke Anna as she turned back to face Lawrence. Lifting the movie script out of the trash can, she tore the pages from the binding and threw them at Lawrence. "Eat that Mr. Lawrence — I mean, Chase."

"Anna," Lawrence said, "I created you! Without your mentor you are nothing! You'll flop in Doug Fairbanks's movie. Only I, Chase Lawrence, can make you shine! You'll be back in your parents' laundry cleaning the vomit and shit off the gwah los' clothes that you despise. Don't leave me!" pleaded Lawrence as Fairbanks slammed the door behind them.

For the next three months, Anna was cast in the swashbuckling Fairbanks fantasy film *The Thief of Baghdad,* playing the role of a Mongolian slave girl. At the gala event for the premiere of the film, Anna looked truly exquisite in a slinky, black silk Chinese cheongsam, escorted by Douglas Fairbanks on one arm and Lillian Gish on the other.

At the end of the film, Anna and the other principal players received a zealous standing ovation. As they exited the theater with Fairbanks and Gish, they were greeted by a gauntlet of adoring fans. Anna had encountered enthusiastic fans on previous occasions, but never to such massive numbers of admirers, both white and Chinese. She felt overwhelmed by so much attention. Frantically, she scribbled her autograph over and over for the swarming fans. With the aid of security guards, she finally reached a waiting Rolls Royce, accompanied by Fairbanks, his wife Mary Pickford, and Lillian Gish.

"Whew! Welcome to show biz, Anna," laughed Gish as she gazed into a compact mirror to smooth her ruffled hair.

Pickford squeezed Anna's hand. "My dear, there is an old saying. Perhaps your people have a version of it. 'Don't wish too hard for something, you might get what you want.'"

Anna looked at Pickford with puzzlement.

"Mary, cut the bullshit," Gish said. "Anna, she meant getting what you really want is no guarantee of happiness. In fact, you might shed more tears over answered prayers than unanswered prayers." She chuckled. "Which is nonsense. I am a successful movie actress and I have always been happy."

Mary squeezed Anna's hand even more tightly. "Anna dear, I suppose Lilly is right. No doubt you will have a long and rewarding acting career. My apologies, my friend."

Anna responded with a forced smile, apprehensive of what the future might bring.

After the premiere, Fairbanks and Pickford had arranged an extravagant party at the Pickfair Mansion with all of Hollywood's elite invited. The guests were greeted by dazzling fireworks and the blowing of trumpets by men dressed in Roman togas. At the entrance to the mansion stood a tall, handsome Asian man dressed in a tailored tuxedo.

"Anna, it would be so gauche to enter a celebration that honors your first featured film without being escorted by a handsome man," Fairbanks said. "Anna May Wong, it is my great pleasure to introduce you to another pioneer, who is breaking the race barriers of the film industry. Meet Mr. Sessue Hayakawa."

"Now, you two kids behave yourselves," joked Pickford.

Hayakawa politely kissed Anna's hand. "What a divine honor to at last meet the great Anna May Wong, the only Chinese actor or actress to receive top billing in a gai jin flicker."

"A what?" asked Anna.

Hayakawa began to laugh. "Miss Wong, I believe you Chinese have two terms for white people, lo fon and gwah lo, both of which have derogatory connotations. We Japanese call the whites gai jin, although the term literally means *foreigner*. That too is meant as a slight toward the white sons-of-bitches." With that said, the Japanese man took hold of Anna's arm to escort her into the Pickfair ballroom.

Anna felt a bit shy walking arm-in-arm with the handsome Japanese actor. She had heard of him. His fame preceded him. But, unlike most, if not all Asian actors in America, Hayakawa was cast in starring roles.

"The honorable Miss Anna May Wong and the honorable Mr. Sessue Hayakawa!" announced the Fairbanks head butler to the other guests in the grand ballroom.

Anna was giddily euphoric over the ostentatious display of wealth and influence. Gold confetti and colored ribbons rained down on Anna and the other guests. Half-naked women swung from lead-glass chandeliers, and a thirty-piece orchestra played blaring jazz music. A ten-layer cake sat in the center of the room, and an attractive servant girl offered Anna and Hayakawa glasses of champagne from a gold tray.

"Are we having fun yet?" whispered Hayakawa playfully. "Anna, you are the prettiest woman in this room full of pretty women."

Though now a grown woman, Anna blushed from the man's compliment like a smitten schoolgirl. But before she could respond, a dozen young starlets mobbed Hayakawa, pulling him away from Anna. Anna watched with amazement as each young girl fought for Hayakawa's attention, grabbing his arms and trying to steal a kiss. Anna felt a flash of anger, not only because the Japanese actor she was taken with had been spirited away, but because she herself did not draw the same outrageous attention from the men in the room. She swallowed the contents of the champagne glass, then snatched two more glasses from a servant passing by.

"Whoa there, partner. Too much of that fire water will get your head in a bucket," came a voice she had not heard in some years. Pivoting quickly, she was astounded to see a tall, lanky, handsome white man. Her lips curved into a smile.

"Marion? Or is it Duke? My childhood knight in shining armor, you saved me from many a bully!" cried Anna hugging her old friend.

"My Celestial sister, I will always be there to slay your dragons. By the way, I am no longer addressed as Marion Morrison. 'The Duke' is fine, but I now go by the more rugged name of John Wayne. The gods atop Mount Hollywood think John Wayne is a more catchy name for a movie star than Marion Morrison. I reckon they're the ones sending me the paychecks, so I am now Mr. Wayne. But you can still call me Duke, old friend."

Anna smiled warmly. "Duke, my hero. I think I saw you a few times in those one-reelers, but I didn't connect the name with the face. I am so proud of you," spoke Anna as she continued to hug her old friend.

"Anna, I'm not at the top of the totem pole yet. I'm making low-budget potboilers, but like you, we are destined for big things. My friend, the director John Ford, recommended me to his colleague Raoul Walsh for a big-budget Western called *The Big Trail.* I believe he's the same fella that directed you in *Baghdad.*"

"Congrats—" Anna stopped her sentence when she spotted Priscilla Lawrence eyeing her from a corner of the room. Remembering the closeness she'd once felt for Priscilla, Anna felt obligated to speak to her. "Duke, I love you dearly, but I see someone I must speak to," said Anna, planting a kiss on Wayne's cheek and stepping away quickly.

"See ya in the movies, old friend!" shouted Wayne through cupped hands.

Anna waved and blew him a kiss as she walked across the crowded room.

11

Anna greeted Priscilla with an awkward hello. The two women hugged each other stiffly.

"Anna, I congratulate you on your debut film. You earned it," said Pricilla. "Can we speak in private?"

Anna nodded. Pricilla led Anna out onto the balcony for more privacy.

"Cilla, considering the ugliness between Chase and Mr. Fairbanks, I'm surprised he invited you to the party."

Priscilla chuckled. "Dear girl, neither Doug or Mary invited me to this pretentious party, I invited myself." Priscilla placed a cigarette in her mouth to lessen the stress of the moment.

"I could use a cigarette, too, Cilla," requested Anna.

Priscilla placed another cigarette in her mouth, lit the two cigarettes, then handed one to Anna.

"Something on your mind, Cilla?" Anna asked, blowing smoke out the side of her mouth.

Priscilla appeared to be fighting back tears. "Anna, my darling, I was like a mother to you. Why did you abandon me?"

Anna shrugged her shoulders, struggling for a response. Their eyes locked.

"Cilla, I love you so much, and yes, you have been like a mother to me, but I had to move on. Your husband would not allow me to appear in Doug Fairbanks's movie. I had to cut the cord to become what I dreamed of becoming."

Priscilla appeared to grow agitated. "All right, my daughter. Your goddamn name is now on theater marquees, and for that you ignore me. Come back to the Lawrence mansion. We need each other."

Anna rolled her eyes. "Cilla, please. You know that would be so outrageous for me to move back in with you. I came close to kicking Chase in the family jewels the last time we met! I refuse to live with the bastard, as if he would want me, anyway. Good-bye, Cilla."

"So that's it? Is that what you want for me, to die alone surrounded by marble statues and gold-plated toilet seats? Chase will not give me a divorce, and even if he did, I have no skills. I am now too old to play a beautiful ingénue."

"Cilla, I don't even communicate with my blood parents. Like my parents, you don't understand my needs. I said good-bye. Don't make me keep repeating that," stated Anna with a cold detachment.

Priscilla flicked her lit cigarette at Anna. It bounced off her chest in a shower of sparks. Unfazed, Anna showed no reaction. Then Priscilla stormed away. Anna continued to stand on the balcony and watched Priscilla walk across the street to her own mansion. Anna displayed no emotion as she wrestled with her conscience. She reflected on the silly, fun times she'd had with Cilla. "I'm sorry, Cilla, that I hurt you so much, but I want to climb the Gold Mountain and not you or anyone else will hold me back," she mouthed to herself.

Anna left the balcony and returned to the party. She drank several glasses of champagne and danced giddily with a number of revelers, both male and female. She became mesmerized by the brilliant lights and the loud music. The maddening energy of the beautiful people around her intoxicated her far beyond the liquor.

This is where I belong, she thought as she danced, her body entwined with a beautiful female starlet. *This is what I earned for myself.*

"May I cut in?" spoke a handsome gwah lo man.

"Dax!" cried Anna as the man rudely pushed the other woman aside. Dax took Anna in his arms for a slow dance.

"I am seeing a lot of old acquaintances this evening," remarked

Anna.

Dax chuckled. "Anyone who is anyone, that is if he or she has good sense, will attend a party held by Fairbanks and Pickford. And I play an important part of the history of the great Anna May Wong," quipped Dax.

"How is that?" Anna replied.

"I was your very first celluloid kiss...and it will not be the last," murmured Dax. He kissed Anna softly on the lips.

"Excuse me, Dax, I wish to cut in," voiced Sessue, tapping Dax on the shoulder.

Glaring at Sessue, and clearly agitated, Dax snapped, "Don't you have some raw fish to slice, or perhaps you could use your sushi knife to slit your throat."

Sessue returned the agitated gaze. "Dax, your mother called. It's time for your evening bottle."

Dax let go of Anna. With seething anger, he prepared to take a punch at the sarcastic Japanese man. Quickly, Anna stood between the two men just as Sessue was about to throw his own punch at the German actor.

"Uh, Sessue and I were about to discuss my role in his next movie. We will speak again soon, I promise you, Dax," Anna said.

Dax appeared confused by Anna's intentions. "So be it, go kiss your Jap friend's ass," he barked as he stormed away.

"Anna May, I thank you for coming to the defense of a yellow brother," Sessue said.

Anna was quite amused by his remark. "My yellow brother, I didn't come to your defense, I just wanted to avoid an ugly scene that would spoil the festivities."

"In any case, it was well played. Now, let us find a private location so we can discuss our movie."

"I only made that up to stop the fight."

"Of course, but since you mentioned it, it sounds like an interesting idea. Come with me," voiced Sessue as he led her to the empty dining room. Along the way, he lifted one of the champagne bottles from an ice bucket, along with two glasses. After they had entered the dimly lit dining room, Sessue closed the door. He wedged a chair under the doorknob to ensure their privacy.

"Dom Pérignon, 1917, a very good year," said Sessue as he pulled the cork. "Sit down, Anna May Wong." He poured them both glasses of the vintage champagne.

"What happened to all those pretty gwah lo bitches that were clinging to you like leeches?" asked Anna.

"Those gai jin bimbos are only a pleasant diversion, like near-beer. It quenches the thirst but has little body and taste," laughed Sessue as he gently took the champagne glass from Anna's hand. Sensually, he embraced her and kissed her with intense passion.

Anna's heart began to race and her face flushed. "Mr. Hayakawa, I am a virgin. I am not sure I am ready for your advances."

Sessue laughed absurdly, "Anna May Wong, the sexy siren of the silver screen, is a virgin? This is like learning that Rudolph Valentino is a virgin. If you plan on playing the femme fatale, you'd better get some practice in." He slipped his hand through the slit of her silk dress to rub her private parts.

Breathing heavily, Anna began to perspire. "No...no..." whispered Anna meekly.

"Two yellow people...do we not make a good team?" murmured Sessue as he lifted her neck and nibbled on her ear.

Anna had kissed many men in her movies, but it was only acting, and both she and the male actors were being paid. There was no romance in it. But this time the kisses from Sessue were genuine. Slowly, he unbuttoned the front of her dress and began rubbing her breasts. Anna had never felt such ecstasy. She lost all of her inhibitions and was giving herself to Sessue. Sessue had just begun to remove her dress when the intimate moment was interrupted by a loud banging on the door.

"Miss Wong! Miss Wong! Are you in there?" cried a distraught voice.

Swiftly, Anna redressed, then assisted Sessue with his tuxedo jacket.

"What the hell do you want? I am discussing a movie deal with Mr. Hayakawa," she screeched.

Anna removed the chair that blocked the door and yanked the door open. Confused, Anna and Sessue saw a very excited servant standing before them.

"Miss Wong, I beg your pardon for the interruption. There has been a terrible accident. Mrs. Lawrence accidentally shot herself. She is asking for you."

The lively music had stopped and most of the guests were no longer present. The ballroom felt eerie. Anna and Sessue ran outside hand-in-hand. Many of the guests were standing on the terrace, gazing across the street at the Lawrence mansion.

"Sorry, Sessue, I have to see what has happened to Cilla," cried Anna, kissing him on the cheek. She raced down the driveway toward the Lawrence mansion.

Anna was greeted by a chaotic scene of police cars and an ambulance, complete with flashing lights. Dozens of onlookers had walked over from the Fairbanks and Pickford party. Pushing and shoving her way into the mansion foyer, to her horror, Anna found the dying Priscilla being lifted onto a gurney. Her chest was covered with bandages soaked with bright-red blood.

"Chink, get your ass back. We've got to take Mrs. Lawrence to the hospital without a moment to waste," said one of the police officers. He pinned Anna's arms back as she struggled to be near Priscilla.

"Sons-of-bitches, let Miss Wong go. It's her I want to see," said Cilla weakly. "And what's the hurry? I'll be dead before you can get me to the hospital anyway."

The policeman released Anna. She rushed to Priscilla's side. Crying uncontrollably, she placed her cheek on Priscilla's chest, ignoring the blood. "Cilla, did you take your life because of me?"

Priscilla reached out with her bloody hand to touch Anna's face. "No, my daughter. I was just tired of living. Don't let us gwah lo bastards take advantage of you," spoke Priscilla in a labored voice.

Anna reached down to kiss Priscilla on the lips "Cilla, I am so sorry for not being a better friend and daughter."

Priscilla smiled at Anna, as if to say in silent words, *It's okay, now I will have no more pain and suffering.* Priscilla chuckled meekly. "I was wrong, my daughter. I will not die alone..." she mouthed before closing her eyes.

The doctor placed his stethoscope on Priscilla's chest. "Mrs. Lawrence was correct. She will no longer suffer. I am sorry to inform you, Miss Wong, that Mrs. Lawrence has passed on."

"Cilla, you were my mother and I am your daughter," mouthed Anna as she touched Priscilla's lips with her fingers.

"Bravo! Bravo! A performance worthy of that new acting award called the Oscar," exclaimed Chase. "Bravo! Indeed, how many others did you have to step on to become a movie star?"

Anna looked up at Chase, her eyes burning with contempt. She lunged at him, kicking and clawing at him savagely. The two police officers pulled Anna off the man.

Chase's face was bleeding and scratched from the assault. Pulling a silk handkerchief from his suit pocket, he wiped the blood from his face with a hateful laugh. "You slit-eyed whore. You're no actress. Next year you'll be serving champagne at Pickfair instead of being served it. You're nothing!" screeched Chase. "Get off my property, now!"

Anna yanked her arms away from the policemen's grip. "It's all right, officers, I won't hurt the precious gwah lo director any further," she sneered. She waded through the bystanders.

"Honey," called a concerned Mary Pickford from the crowd, "come back to Pickfair."

Ignoring her, Anna left the mansion.

For several hours, Anna walked aimlessly on the streets. She sat on a bench and lit a cigarette. She gazed at the enormous Hollywood sign, newly erected on a hill overlooking the Los Angeles basin and illuminated by powerful Klieg lights.

"Was that bastard Chase Lawrence right? Will I be a servant next year in the mansions where I was once a welcome guest?" murmured Anna, inhaling and exhaling cigarette smoke.

Instead of returning to the Gish mansion, where Lillian had invited her to stay as long as she wished, she walked to her parents' laundry, still wearing the slinky black silk cheongsam, now torn and sweat-stained. Her feet ached from walking in her high-heel, formal dress shoes. She removed them and walked barefoot for the remaining two miles to her parents' residence.

Disheveled and exhausted, Anna walked into the ground floor, the family laundry. As usual, her parents and employees were diligently cleaning and ironing the customers' clothing. The Chinese employees who had known Anna since she was an infant embraced her and cheered her recent acting accomplishments.

"Anna! Anna!" came the collective cheers from the laundry workers.

"Enough!" screeched Sam Sing. "You are not being paid to applaud and hug my daughter. Get back to work, now!"

Weeping, Anna's mother hugged her warmly. "Welcome home, my beautiful daughter. You are now a famous screen actress. Your father and I are so proud of you." She looked Anna over and noticed the blood smudges on her face and hands. "What happened to you? Are you hurt?"

Before Anna could reply, her father barked, "Aren't you lowering yourself? The famous Anna May Wong, visiting her peasant parents. Aren't you afraid you might get some grime on your fancy dress?"

"Husband, that is enough. Can you not tell from her appearance that something terrible has happened to her?"

Deep guilt welled up inside Anna as tears ran down her blood-caked face.

"It's all right, my daughter. You need not explain yourself at this time. For now, you need a hot bath, hot food, and rest."

"My wife, don't you think the movie star would be slumming by sleeping above a lowly laundry?" spoke Sam Sing with biting contempt.

"Shut up!" shouted Lee You. "Anna is our daughter. Whatever she did or did not do can be forgiven. She is our own flesh and blood."

Lee You led Anna upstairs as Sam Sing returned to work, mumbling expletives to himself. For the next two days, Anna remained in the bedroom, drinking whiskey by bribing the laundry employees to sneak her bottles. At the same time, she refused little food that her mother had prepared for her.

For Anna, time seemed to move as slowly as a broken clock. She refused to see Douglas Fairbanks, Mary Pickford, or Lillian Gish.

"I killed Cilla. She treated me with nothing but kindness. If there is a hell, I deserve to spend eternity there," Anna murmured to herself. Swallowing the last drops of what remained in one of her whiskey bottles, she smashed it against the nightstand. The bottle shattered into a thousand pieces across the floor. On her knees, Anna sorted through the numerous pieces of broken glass. She found one that was long and sharp, and ran the edge across her index finger. Bright-red blood dripped steadily from her fingertip.

"Chase Lawrence was right, I am nothing," whispered Anna to herself. She then pressed the broken shard of glass against her left wrist, sliding it across her wrist while pressing downward forcibly. Blood began to spurt out. With a contented smile, Anna lay on her bed. Delirious, she returned to the night when she and Priscilla had playfully gone swimming naked in the Roman-style swimming pool. She envisioned a joyous Priscilla kissing her on the lips and whispering in her ear that she had forgiven her. She then drifted into unconsciousness.

12

A nna felt a gentle nudge on her shoulder. She awakened to a bright light emanating from a bare bulb on a ceiling. She saw blurred faces standing over her. As her eyes focused, Anna saw her parents, a doctor, and Hayakawa. She had no idea how much time had passed.

"Oh, Anna, you're awake. We were so worried about you," voiced her mother.

"I thank the Lord Buddha for saving you," added Hayakawa.

The doctor lifted Anna's uninjured right wrist to check her pulse. "The pulse rate is normal. Miss Wong should be as good as new in no time, Mr. and Mrs. Wong. I regret I must inform the authorities. As a physician, I am obligated by law to inform the police of any self-inflicted injury. I am sorry."

Hayakawa grabbed the doctor by his coat. "You jackass gai jin, don't you know who Miss Wong is? She is a famous movie actress. Can you imagine what negative publicity could do to her career?" he exclaimed, shaking the doctor fiercely.

"Take your damn hands off me, you damn Jap," the doctor replied, swatting Hayakawa's hands away. The doctor shook his head, looking sympathetically had Anna. "Yes, yes, I am aware of who Miss Wong is. My kids are fans of hers. They've told me how much they loved Miss Wong in *The Thief of Bagdad.*" He sighed as he wrote a few notes in Anna's chart. "Very well, in my report I will write that Miss Wong accidentally cut herself while slicing a cabbage. Fair enough?"

Lee You hugged the doctor. Hayakawa shook the doctor's hand.

Anna's father stood by silently.

"Thank you so much, sir, for saving Anna's life and her career," spoke a relieved Hayakawa. "Doug, Mary, and Lilly are all waiting outside. They're dying to welcome you back to where you belong," added Hayakawa with a wide grin. He chuckled. "Sorry...I suppose *dying* was a bad choice of words. You are among the living and you have too many things to accomplish before you leave this world."

While Anna remained in the hospital to recuperate for another ten days, she was visited every day by her mother and Hayakawa, who would recite lines from Shakespearean plays to her. There were also frequent visits by Fairbanks, Pickford, and Gish. The one person who didn't visit was her father, who was still embittered by his daughter's nonconformity to Chinese tradition and her rebellious temperament.

On her last day in the hospital, Sessue asked to speak to Anna privately. A "Do Not Enter" sign was placed on the outside of her hospital room door. Sessue pulled a chair beside Anna's bed. He took a flask of strong whiskey from his inside coat pocket and poured a good measure of the liquor into a glass.

"Anna dear, I think you now have your head on straight," he quipped as he handed her the glass.

Anna smiled gleefully as she gulped down the whiskey. She held out the glass for more of the potent liquor. "It's all the medicine I really need," she giggled. "You have honored me with your presence every day that I've been in the hospital. In fact, your face was one of the first things that I saw when I regained consciousness. What do you want? I don't think you're going to all this trouble just so I can be your bed partner. You have all those pimple-faced gwah lo girls beating down the door to feed your sexual appetite."

Sessue laughed. "So true, Miss Wong. I have to fight off the gai jin bimbos with a stick. Actually, I am asking you to make a series of movies with me. Together we will make history."

Ana looked away in reflection. After a long pause, her eyes returned to Sessue. "Sessue, am I worthy of being in your flickers? I do not believe I am even worth living. I killed Cilla by turning my back to her."

Sessue began to rant in Japanese, then kissed Anna on the lips. "Silly Chinese girl. Cilla was sick in the head. Her demons killed her, not you. Cilla was Cilla. If she hadn't taken her life a couple of weeks ago, it would have been next month, next year, or whenever. That's the kind of crazy gai jin woman she was. Forget about Priscilla and Chase Lawrence and get on with your goddamn life."

Anna stared at Sessue, soaking up what he said.

"I beg you, Anna, please. Promise you will not try to take your life again. We all have our demons to battle. You just need to learn to cope."

Anna placed an appreciative hand on Sessue's cheek. "Tell me, what is our first movie together about?" she asked, having made peace with herself—at least for the time being.

With giddy excitement, Sessue pulled out a number of story concepts from an attaché case he had brought with him. He rang the buzzer to request that the nurse bring them a pot of hot tea. For several hours they discussed movie scripts, with Anna throwing in a few ideas of her own for their possible collaboration.

After her release from the hospital, Anna returned to the Gish mansion, with Sessue visiting daily to rehearse their first film together. Only two weeks after her release from the hospital, Anna was well enough to play Sessue's love interest, as she would do in several films to come with Hayakawa.

She asked Sessue one day, "Do you plan to lock me in my dressing room between takes?"

Sessue appeared confused, uncertain whether Anna's odd statement was in jest or serious. "What do you mean?"

Anna giggled "The first half-dozen flickers I was in, I was locked in my dressing room between takes for my own safety. But I felt more like a prisoner than being protected. It was only sometime later that I found out it was my father's idea. According to my dear father, it was to protect me against the evil gwah lo men who might want to have their way with me." Anna began to laugh. "In truth, my dear father just didn't want me to pollute my mind with the gwah lo way of thinking. The patriarch Sam Sing would have had a fit if I became a banana. That means—"

Sessue covered her mouth. "Dear girl, you need not explain. I also have yellow skin. My friends and relatives have labeled me as a banana—yellow on the outside, white on the inside."

And so began a long series of successful films that Anna and Sessue collaborated on. Like Sessue, Anna earned a considerably high income for anyone, yellow or white. She moved out of the Gish mansion and into a grand home she leased not far from the magnificent mansions of Gish and Pickfair. Sessue was a frequent visitor. Like most expensive homes in Beverly Hills, Anna's had a splendid marble swimming pool. After rehearsing scenes for whatever particular film they might be working on, the two of them would take a pleasant dip in the pool. A black maid would bring them glasses of tequila in crushed ice and expensive Beluga caviar.

Anna had never been so deliriously happy in her young life.

"You're riding a wave, Anna. Try to ride the crest as long as you can," remarked Hayakawa.

Anna grinned while sitting on his lap. She swallowed a shot of tequila, then bit into a slice of lime. She gazed at the beautiful surroundings of her leased mansion. "Isn't it marvelous, Sessue, to be young, rich, and famous?" she said.

Sessue took the slice of lime from Anna's hand and bit into it. "Certainly, my dear. While it lasts."

Sessue stood up and held Anna in his arms. They were wet after their dip in the pool. "Shall we finish something we began at the Pickfair party?" whispered Sessue into Anna's ear.

"While we're still young, rich, and famous," giggled Anna as Sessue carried her to the master bedroom.

Their relationship grew stronger each day, both professionally and personally. With the advent of talking films, several popular actors' careers declined, as they had boring or mundane speaking voices. But Anna's low, husky, exotic voice only enhanced her popularity.

But the high wave, as Sessue predicted, eventually subsided. After a string of successful films, the cold, gray day came when Sessue called Anna to his own mansion, which was a few houses down from hers. Upon entering his office, Anna could clearly see that Sessue had been drinking heavily. A half-empty brandy bottle sat on his desk,

"Is somebody dead?" joked Anna as she poured herself a glass of brandy.

"Yes, the dead man is Sessue Hayakawa, or at least my film career is deceased."

Anna pulled up a chair to sit beside Sessue, who was growing increasingly despondent. "The studio has dropped my contract. I no longer have a net to catch me. The gai jin who manipulate the puppet strings in Hollywood no longer want a Jap on the marquee," he said, and began to sob.

Anna pulled his head to rest against her chest. "Sessue, I don't understand. All of our films have made the studios money. Why would they fire you?"

Sessue sat up to take a swig from the brandy bottle. "Gai jin actors like Doug Fairbanks and Rudolph Valentino earn four times what I earn. I went to the studio and asked for pay equal to theirs. Harry Hightower laughed in my face. He immediately called for his secretary to bring him my contract. He tore it to pieces and threw it at my feet."

"How can he cancel your contract without good reason?" asked Anna.

Sessue chuckled. "Gai jins always have an excuse for breaking contracts. If they do not have one, they will make one up. Being a dumb Jap, I did not bother to read the fine print. There is a morality clause. The studio head knew I was having sex with gai jin women. They were of legal age, but for a 'yellow nigger' to have sex with a white woman is an effrontery against God."

101

Anna embraced him. "Oh, Sessue you should have left well enough alone. You were making more money than most gwah lo men on the Gold Mountain. You live in a beautiful home. What more do you need?"

Sessue pushed Anna away to gaze out at his well-manicured gardens. "It's the goddamn principle. To be paid even a penny less than gai jin men is to say I am inferior to them."

Anna placed her hand on Sessue's shoulder. "Sessue, you just informed me that you bed gwah lo girls. Do you feel inferior bedding me?"

The direct question put Sessue on the spot. He was embarrassed to look her in the eyes. "Sorry, my dear, perhaps I am inferior to gai jins. If a lowly yellow man receives offers from beautiful gai jin women to bed them, it is like Eve in paradise being offered the sweet apple. How can one say no?"

"I will spell it out for you. N and O—NO! The only reason we are inferior is because the gwah los tell us we are inferior. You have to sleep with gwah lo bitches to make you feel like a man? Sayonara, Sessue."

Anna stormed away. Sessue said nothing as he tried to absorb Anna's words.

Upon returning to her mansion, Anna slumped down on a lawn chair on the terrace. She called for a servant girl to bring her a bottle of whiskey that was bottled in 1905, the year she was born. Kicking off her shoes, she poured the aged liquor into an eighteen-carat-gold goblet that had been gifted to her from Sessue. Sitting up, Anna surveyed the spacious grounds. She reflected on her first starring role in *The Toll of the Sea*—one of the first Hollywood films shot in Technicolor. Inspired by the Madame Butterfly story, she played a Chinese maiden who rescued a young gwah lo man washed ashore. "The gwah lo son-of-a-bitch got me pregnant and I ended up committing suicide. How ridiculous! He wasn't that cute," giggled Anna. "My home is so beautiful. So beautiful! I don't want to give it up. I want to enjoy it fully. It will not last, according to

Sessue."Anna drank the hard liquor until she passed out.

Shortly after Hayakawa's release from his contract, Anna learned that he had fled to Europe, where the film studios and directors were more enlightened and treated minority actors respectfully and granted them non-stereotypical roles.

Fearful that her career might be damaged by the loss of her colleague, Anna nonetheless continued to have steady work in films, although she was most often typecast as the tragic heroine or temptress. She yearned for more dramatic, challenging roles, but a number of significant roles that should have gone to Anna still went to heavily made-up Caucasian actresses. One such gwah lo actress— a perky redhead named Myrna Loy—was increasingly cast in roles that should have gone to Anna. Anna began to drink more to soothe her bitterness over her lack of being cast in good, meaningful roles. When she complained about it to casting directors, producers, and even the studio head, they would usually respond with the excuse that they were only following the casting system, and that there were no Asian actors with enough talent to play characters who were Asian.

After one such conversation, Anna laughed bitterly in the studio head's face. "Harry, you gave roles that belong to me to that redhead bitch Myrna Loy. I hope she was a good lay," she remarked cruelly, knowing it was not likely Loy had bedded anyone so she could get particular roles.

"Goddamn yellow bitch, I tried to take care of you as best I could. It's all that old Eastern money. Those bastards do not care about giving 'darkies' like you a decent break. They only understand money. So what if a dumb redhead wears a black wig and has her eyes glued back to make them narrow slits? It's only business. We're not trying to slight the entire Asian race. It's a goddamned business. Now get the hell out of my office!"

Anna knew her harsh criticism of the studio head and the racist casting system prevalent in Hollywood would have negative repercussions to her career. But she spoke out nonetheless. "I am tired of the bullshit hypocrisy," murmured Anna as she left the office.

No doubt out of spite, the studio cast Anna in a Myrna Loy film called *The Crimson City.* It was a supporting role to Loy, who portrayed a Chinese temptress. It was particularly hurtful to Anna that, standing five foot seven, it was required that the much shorter Loy stood on a wooden fruit crate in her close-up scenes with Anna, making it appear that Loy was taller.

Anna's income became smaller and her roles fewer. She was forced to move from her beloved mansion into a small, one-bedroom flat in downtown Los Angeles.

On her last day before relocating to her flat, she gave her three servants a substantial amount of severance pay — money she could scarcely afford. She swam nude in the mansion pool and consumed an entire bottle of vintage Dom Pérignon that was gifted to her by Douglas Fairbanks after completing her first starring role in *The Thief of Bagdad.*

Noticing that Anna was feeling the effects of the champagne, her servants assisted her in dressing and packing her things. While everyone sobbed heavily, Anna embraced her former domestic help before boarding a taxi for transportation to her new residence, which was situated in a seedy, low-income section of the city. With stubborn, fierce pride, Anna had refused offers to move back in with Gish, Fairbanks, and even her parents.

Upon arriving at the dilapidated apartment building, Anna stumbled out of the taxi, still drunk from the champagne. Fishing through her pockets to find enough money to pay the taxi driver, she was stunned to find the rolls of money that she had given to her servants. Amazed by their generosity, Anna handed a dollar to the taxi driver, then dropped to her knees, sobbing. "My help slipped the money I gave them into my pocket when I hugged them. They knew I was hurting financially. What beautiful souls. They need the money as much as I do. When my star begins to shine, I promise you I will pay you back, my beloved friends."

"Look! It's Anna May Wong!" screamed a mixed group of gwah lo and Chinese women walking by. The giddy young women began to paw at her and begged for her autograph.

Standing up, Anna tried to maintain her composure after consuming so much alcohol. The star-struck fans didn't seem to notice her slurred speech and flushed face. Anna smiled warmly as she signed the requested autographs.

"I am your biggest fan, Miss Wong. You were so awesome in *Toll of the Sea*, though I don't think you should have killed yourself over that jerk sailor who got you pregnant," enthused one fan.

All of the women, including Anna, erupted in laughter at the fan's amusing remark.

"Miss Wong, what brings you to this dumpy part of L.A.? Are you doing research for an upcoming role?" asked another female fan.

The fans bitterly reminded Anna of her dramatic drop in star status. Embarrassed and angry, Anna began to tear up the autographs she had just signed. "You little zit-faced teenagers! Get the hell out of my sight. I am a busy woman. I have no time for such nonsense."

The young women stood in shock at their idol's angry outburst.

"Excuse me," one of them said sarcastically. "Our apologies for disturbing the great Anna May Wong. We apologize for breathing the same air as you."

The young women tore up the autographs Anna had missed and threw them in her face.

"Come on, girls, maybe we can catch Myrna Loy, that other Chinese actress, for an autograph," voiced one of the girls, unaware that Loy was a white woman made-up to look Asian. "She's a better actress, anyway."

"I am Anna May Wong, actress! Myrna Loy is a hack! Mickey Mouse is a better actor, and besides, she is a gwah lo pretending to be me!" shouted Anna at the disgruntled fans.

On weak legs, she carried her two pieces of luggage into the apartment building. The clerk at the front desk sat reading a newspaper. He nodded with indifference as Anna entered. She dropped the suitcases with a loud thud.

The clerk looked up, clearly annoyed. "Well, what the hell do you want, China lady?"

"Kind sir, I live on the fourth floor. Would you or an assistant be kind enough to carry my bags to my apartment?"

The clerk laughed, greatly amused. "What do you think this place is, the Beverly Hills Hotel?" He went back to his newspaper and ignored Anna as she stood there.

Still intoxicated, Anna stood rigidly with the air of an aristocrat. "You gwah lo son-of-a-bitch, do you know who I am?"

"I don't give a shit if you're the Empress of China. In this dung heap, you carry your own bags."

Anna cursed at the man in Chinese. Lifting her suitcases, she staggered up the four flights of stairs to her modest flat. Fighting for breath, she saw a letter lying on the floor at her apartment door. It was addressed to her from a film studio called Fairmont Productions. With giddy excitement, Anna entered the flat and hurriedly opened the letter. *I am going to be a star again!* she thought.

The letter was an offer to appear in their production called *The Dragon Horse*. She would be the lead female character in the film and would be paid five hundred dollars.

"Five hundred dollars?" she shrieked indignantly. "Insolent assholes. I've spent five hundred on a single dress!" She threw the letter into the trash and opened a bottle of far cheaper whiskey than she was accustomed to. She noticed a cockroach scampering across the floor. Anna threw the bottle at the annoying bug. Whiskey and shards of glass exploded across the walls and floor, and the commotion caused dozens more cockroaches to scurry in every direction around the small room.

Anna sat on the floor, ignoring that her clothes were soaked by the whiskey that covered the floor. Tears welled up in her eyes as she fished the offer for the film role out of the trash.

13

To save money, Anna walked the six miles to the warehouse that was a makeshift film set, rather than spend fifty cents for a taxi, or even a nickel for the city bus.

After arriving at the address, she was taken aback to see a cardboard sign attached to the entrance of the warehouse, and on it was sloppily written "Fairmont Film Productions."

She entered the warehouse and saw the usual chaotic bustle of film crew workers busily setting up for the next scene, but unlike the big-budget film sets Anna was accustomed to, all the film crew and actors were Asian, and the props and painted backdrops were made of low-cost materials.

A short, squatty Chinese man approached her. "Anna May Wong! We were expecting you. Welcome to Fairmont Studios. I am the director and head of the studio, Pun Yee. Here is the script. Take a few minutes to go over your part,"

Anna was overwhelmed by the entire situation. "Mr. Yee...or is it Pun? Do you go by the Chinese custom of first name last, last name first?"

The man laughed. He looked like he hadn't shaved for several days and his breath reeked of cheap wine. He guided Anna to a canvas folding chair. "Anna, babe, just call me boss. Sit your ass down," he ordered.

Anna did as she was told. An elderly woman came forward to apply make-up on Anna's face.

"Where is my dressing room?" Anna asked. "I will need more time to prepare for my role than just a few minutes."

107

"You're sitting in your dressing room," the director laughed. "What do you think this is, Universal Studios? Fairmont makes flickers to cater to the Chinese community. All the actors are Chinese. No different than those all-black films that cater to blacks, or hak gwais, as we Chinese call them. And another thing, Miss Wong. Who needs rehearsing or preparation? This is not Shakespeare." Pun Yee laughed.

"Shit, I need the money," mouthed Anna under her breath.

"What did you say, Miss Wong?"

"I said, how did you find me?"

Yee shook his head, grinning in a silly manner "Miss Wong, news in Hollywood travels fast. One day you're riding high on the Gold Mountain, the next day you're in the shithole. We just checked every dive in L.A. till we found you. Miss Anna May Wong, welcome to the real world. If the gwah los didn't need someone to serve them coffee and dainty little sandwiches and to clean their clothes, they would have no use for chinks at all. Remember who you are—an actress who entertains people. You are at least entertaining your own kind," declared Yee.

Anna sat speechless as the make-up artist continued to apply make-up to her face. She knew that, as rude as Pun Yee's words were, they had a ring of truth to them.

"I am ready when you are, boss," stated Anna, having accepted the situation for the time being.

And so began a series of undistinguished films Anna acted in. At times, Anna would show up on the set drunk, but being a skillful actress, few people could tell she was inebriated during her performances. Out of pride, she refused to see her show business friends Douglas Fairbanks, Mary Pickford, and Lillian Gish. She also denied visits from her mother on the film sets and at the apartment building where she resided.

One evening, after another long day of shooting in one of several B-movies, she staggered up the stairs to her flat, drinking whiskey from a flask. Fumbling with the key, she finally managed to open the door. Anna screeched in shock to see Gish and Dax sitting in her tiny, one-room dwelling.

Gish leaped off the chair to embrace her.

"How did you get in, Auntie Lilly?"

Dax rubbed his fingers together. "Money can open a lot of doors. Lilly slipped the desk clerk five dollars to let us in," he replied.

Gish snatched the flask of whiskey from Anna's hand. "My dear, you don't need that," spoke Gish as Dax poured her a cup of hot coffee from a thermos they had brought with them. "Please sit with us."

Sitting down, Anna drank the hot coffee with trembling hands. "Please go. I am a busy woman, Auntie Lilly," murmured Anna, deeply embarrassed that Gish and Dax had seen her living in squalor and taking to the bottle.

"No," Gish said matter-of-factly. "Dax and I will not leave till you hear us out. Anna, I'm sad that you need tough love. If I may speak frankly, you look like shit. You're a lost Chinese girl out of control."

"Lilly and I would like to help you. We want to pull you out of the nightmare you are now in," Dax said gently. "I beg you, let Lilly and me pull you up back into the sunlight."

With foolish pride, Anna tossed the coffee in Dax's face. "Get out! I do not need any gwah lo's help. I have plenty of work—all I need."

Gish wiped Dax's face with a handkerchief. "Certainly, girl," she said, her voice rising with frustration. "You get all the work you want acting in low-budget 'flickers,' as you call them, made by fly-by-night film studios. I could eat a can of film and puke a better picture."

Dax patted his expensive tailored suit with his own handkerchief. "Anna my friend, I am going to overlook your distasteful act. You are under a great deal of stress. Being an actor is not the easiest way to earn a living, and it's even more difficult for someone of color. Now, sit your ass down and listen to our proposal."

Anna fetched a kitchen towel from a drawer to clean Dax's face, then sat down. "I am sorry, Dax, Auntie Lilly. But you need to walk around in my shoes for a time. I reached the summit of the Gold Mountain, then fell back down. I am so lost and ashamed. I am very sorry, my friends."

Dax pulled an envelope from his inside suit pocket. He opened the envelope to reveal two first-class tickets on a German ocean liner, its destination the German seaport of Hamburg. "Anna dear, together we will take Europe by storm. Your faded star will shine even brighter in Europe, where they embrace people of color. Being of German extraction, I hope to also blossom in my Fatherland." Dax began to laugh oddly. "It appears that Hollywood has no more use for actors with thick German accents than it does people with a yellow tan!" he exclaimed as he dropped the tickets in Anna's lap.

She examined the tickets with puzzlement. "Why do you want to help me after I treated you so badly?"

Both Lilly and Dax laughed.

"Anna," Lilly said. "You're not always the easiest person to get along with. I've said this before, but it bears repeating. You are like the daughter I never had, and like any loving mother, I want my child to succeed."

"And what about you, Dax? You want to get into my panties?" spoke Anna with biting sarcasm.

"Anna, Hollywood can be a lonely city. The whole world, for that matter. On my long journey back to my homeland, it would be nice to have someone to chat with, and to look in awe at the Statue of Liberty with a friend as I say good-bye to America. But I do not need a bed partner. I've had plenty of shallow bed partners to fill my needs for the time being."

Anna sat rather stoically, weighing her options. After a long pause, Anna extended the coffee cup. "I wasted the first cup. May I have more coffee, please? I need to sober up."

Anna drank the hot coffee to clear her mind. After several gulps, she grinned enigmatically. "Germany, huh? Europe is so far away.

Los Angeles is the only home I know." She giggled softly under her breath. "But the gwah los never made me feel like this place was indeed my home. In Germany, I will feel like a stranger, but I am made to feel that way here already. Give me a minute to pack."

"Being a woman of some influence I will make a few calls to speed up the processing of your passport," voiced Gish.

In celebration, Dax drew out his own flask of fine brandy. Filling three glasses, the trio toasted their bold venture.

The day before Anna and Dax were to depart on a charter plane bound for New York City, where they would catch their ship to Germany, Anna paid a visit to her parents to not only bid them farewell, but to also try to mend the lifelong rift between her and her father, and to a lesser extent, her mother.

Anna entered the laundry, and as before, the employees greeted her with tremendous fanfare.

"Anna! Anna!" came the collective shouts of the Chinese employees.

"Shut up and get back to work!" screamed Sam Sing.

The employees quickly returned to work, but not without a warm embrace from Anna first.

"Anna, this is the second time you have disrupted my laundry. Believe it or not, this is a place of business. Unlike you, your mother and I actually *work* for a living."

"Father, Mother, my apologies that I disturbed your work. I am moving to Europe. For how long, I am not sure. I am your daughter. Can you at least sacrifice five minutes of your precious time to say good-bye?"

Sam Sing shook his head. "Very well. The three of us, let's go into my office for some privacy."

As the trio entered the office, Sam Sing slammed the door behind them. "So, my daughter the movie star is starting to dim. Is that why you are moving halfway around the world, to bounce back into the limelight so you can thumb your nose at your family again?"

he snarled.

Lee You slapped her husband's face. "Those were cruel words to say to your own daughter!" she exclaimed.

Anna fought back her tears. "It's all right, Mother. I suppose Father is right. The glamour of being a film actress went to my head. I wanted to not just be equal to the gwah los, I wanted to feel superior to them." Anna laughed in reflection. "When the movie offers from the big studios dried up, I fell off my high horse, but, my parents, I never stopped loving the both of you. I just could never be the kind of traditional Chinese girl that you wanted me to be. We've gone over this many, many times. I want to be an actress. It is all I ever wanted to be."

Sam Sing lifted a bottle of whiskey that sat on his desk and began to take a long swallow. "Damn. What is wrong with this young generation? No respect for tradition, no respect for their elders. What is this world coming to?"

Lee You took a firm grip on her husband's hand. "Husband, I think it is time for change. I have always been the dutiful wife and mother to your children. I wanted to be an opera singer when I was a little girl in China. But I gave up my dream and did what was expected of me by my parents. Your daughter will never be what you want her to be. Yes, Anna is a lowly daughter, but she has your blood and my blood flowing in her veins. She may not have a growth between her legs, but she has the heart of a warrior. Give your daughter at least a small piece of your heart."

Sam Sing took another swig of whiskey, shrugging his shoulders in self-examination. "Acting—what a silly way to earn a living." He sighed. "But you are my daughter. Even if you were a lady of the evening you would still be blood of my blood. Anna, I am a Chinese man. We Chinese men are too proud to show much outward affection, but as your mother says, the world is changing. Perhaps I too need to change. I wish you much good luck in Europe. Whether your star shines again or not, you are still the daughter of Sam Sing." He fought back his tears.

Anna snatched the whiskey bottle from her father and took a long swallow. Then Lee You, who was never much of a drinker, grabbed the bottle from Anna and also took a hearty swig of liquor.

"You will not find good dim sum in Europe," quipped Lee You as the three embraced each other. She shed tears of happiness that her daughter and husband had finally reconciled.

14

Together, the odd couple of Anna and Dax saw the sights of New York City. They rode in a horse-drawn carriage around Central Park. When Anna was refused entry to a few high-end restaurants in the city, they went to New York's Chinatown. Aside from enjoying fine Chinese food, it was a calming interlude to see people of her own heritage before her departure to an uncertain future. After a couple days of restful and joyful sightseeing, Dax and Anna boarded the German ocean liner bound for Germany. She blew a farewell kiss to the Statue of Liberty as the ship left New York Harbor.

On the week-long journey, Anna's lack of feeling for the German actor gradually began to chip away, partly because she had no choice but to trust her traveling companion, as she did not have Gish, her parents, or anyone else to catch her should she have troubles in Europe.

Despite her falling-out with Sessue, she still had an underlying passion for him, but loneliness and facing a world she was unfamiliar with could force anyone to be attached to whoever might be available.

Dax is not an unattractive gwah lo man, thought Anna as they danced together in the ocean liner's ballroom.

Dax gazed passionately into her eyes, then kissed Anna quite sensually. At first, Anna resisted, then gave in to him.

"Anna darling, this is not the first time we have kissed, but the last time I was paid to do it. You may pay me with your future earnings," joked Dax.

114

"I am not sure I can afford you," laughed Anna.

Arm-in-arm, the couple walked outside onto the deck. They gazed at the brilliant silver moon. The shimmering water seemed to extend forever.

"From here I can see Germany and your brilliant future," proclaimed Dax.

The couple nestled together on a reclining deck chair and covered themselves with a thick deck blanket to ward off the evening chill. They held each other, kissing with strong affection. For a moment, time stopped. Finally, Dax lifted Anna in his arms to carry her to their cabin.

Though they shared a cabin together to save on the cost, they did not share a bed, and Dax slept on the floor. But this night was different. Dax confessed that he was very much attracted to Anna. In turn, Anna whispered that she too had a growing attraction to him. Slowly and sensually, the couple undressed each other and shared a bed. Anna had lost her apprehension and anxiety in relocating to another country and people she knew nothing about—at least for the time being.

Dax was only the second man Anna had ever shared a bed with. After making love throughout the night, she got up to smoke a cigarette while Dax slept. She gazed down at Dax's well-developed, athletic body and compared it with Sessue's less muscular body. She laughed softly under her breath when she entertained the thought that Dax was a better lover.

"Is it just reverse racism that I prefer a gwah lo over an Asian man to make myself feel equal to the gwah los?" spoke Anna under her breath.

Upon arriving at the port of Hamburg, Anna's spirits sank when she saw a sooty, drab industrial city instead of the fantasy castles she had envisioned she would see in Europe.

"Cheer up, my love. Hamburg is a polluted city, but you will find Berlin to be far more beautiful and entertaining," said Dax after reading the look on Anna's face.

They took a train to Berlin, which was the film and entertainment capital of Germany. Anna's spirits did indeed rise when she saw that the city was far more attractive and festive than Hamburg.

After a bit of searching, the couple found a modest flat to rent not far from Berlin's film studio complex. Though modest, Anna was delighted to see that the small apartment was clean and not roach-infested like her flat back in Los Angeles.

Once they were settled, the couple immediately traveled to one of Germany's major film studios. Many studio workers and actors greeted Dax warmly, having known him before his departure to America.

"Herr Dax, old friend, you have finally come to your senses and returned to the Fatherland where they make good movies," spoke a middle-aged, rotund, balding man. His eyes immediately turned to Anna. "And who is this beautiful girl?"

"Herr Richard, it is my great honor and pleasure to introduce you to America's most famous Asian female movie actress. I might add that she is also the most popular actress in her native China. She is a direct descendant of Shih Huang-ti, the first emperor of unified China and builder of the Great Wall. This is Anna May Wong."

Anna covered her mouth with her hand, trying to keep a straight face after hearing Dax's outrageous, bald-faced lies.

Eichberg tilted his head one way, then the other. "Um, I have never heard of the great Anna May Wong, but then, I do not pay much attention to the mediocre films made in America."

Anna extended her hand. "Mr. Eichberg, I am honored to meet you. You have not heard of me, but I have heard very much about you. You are Germany's foremost film director. I would be deeply honored act in your films."

Eichberg cackled with amusement. "Fräulein, I do not care if you are the Empress of China. You are without a doubt a beautiful and tall woman with an appealing, exotic look about you. My only concern is, can you act?"

116

Dax took strong offense at Eichberg's reservations about Anna's acting abilities. "Herr Richard, how dare you question Miss Wong's acting talents!"

Anna covered Dax's mouth before he could finish scolding the director.

"Mr. Eichberg—or rather, Herr Eichberg—Dax has been feeding you a line of horse shit to make me appear more important than I am. It is true, I made a few popular movies in America, but like a shooting star, I was only briefly bright until my light faded. And as far as being a major star in China, I have never even been to China, and I am as much related to Emperor Shih Huang-ti as I am to Fu Manchu. I came to Europe to rekindle my career. And lastly, I will give one-hundred-ten-percent effort if you give me a job."

Eichberg looked at Anna, smiling wryly, uncertain what to think of this straight-talking woman. He then burst out in laughter. "Fräulein Wong, I must say, you do have some real brass balls. Meet me here tomorrow at six a.m. for a reading. Do not be late. We Germans like punctuality," he snapped.

The following morning, the director was taken aback to see Anna sitting on the street entrance to the gated film studio. Eichberg stepped out of his chauffeur-driven Mercedes Benz and approached her. "Fräulein Anna, it is five in the morning. I explicitly said six."

Anna lit a cigarette and puffed on it heavily. "Herr Director, if I am to be executed at six, why not just get it over with and kill me now?" spoke Anna enigmatically.

Eichberg gazed at her with puzzlement.

"Herr Director, what I meant is, I live or die by your acceptance to appear in your next film. Reject me and I have nowhere else to go. Your rejection would be the same as an execution," Anna clarified.

Eichberg shook his head. "Fräulein, you are in fact one of a kind, but do not think I will give you work in my next film out of pity. I make important films. There is no room for pity in my line of business."

Eichberg spoke to his chauffeur in German, instructing him to open the car door for Anna. As she entered the back seat, Eichberg ordered the chauffeur to hand him a bottle of schnapps. He unscrewed the cap and handed the bottle to Anna.

"Fräulein, drink, please. It will take the sting out of the cold German morning."

For three hours, Anna read for the film titled *Song*. She auditioned for the role of a down-on-her-luck Malayan dancer who became entangled in a love triangle with a knife-thrower and his partner. After reading her part in the script for the hundredth time, Anna's voice was becoming hoarse. She became quite fatigued after performing a scene repeatedly where she was assaulted by two thugs. Perspiring profusely, Anna collapsed from exhaustion. She awoke to see a German nurse patting her face with a moist face towel and speaking concerned words in German.

"Fräulein Anna, you gave us a good scare."

Eichberg said, "Perhaps this was close to your day of execution, but today is not the day of your death. Rather, it is your rebirth. I am casting you for the lead female role in my next movie, *Song*."

Anna, who had been placed on a couch, sat up and kissed Eichberg with euphoric excitement. "Thank you, thank you, Herr Richard. How long into the audition was it before you decided I was right for the role?" she asked giddily.

Eichberg laughed, "I knew you were correct for the role after the first five minutes of the reading. But we will have to fix that California accent of yours. It's as thick as L.A. smog, which, with your talent, I am certain you will correct."

Anna playfully shook a finger at him. "Why did you keep me hanging for so long?"

"Fräulein Anna, I was interested to see how badly you wanted to work for me. Only someone very committed would put up with the shit I handed you. Welcome aboard, fräulein," stated Eichberg hugging her and kissing her on both cheeks. "

With exuberant joy, Anna rushed to the flat she shared with Dax, to announce the good news.

The couple celebrated with a night on the town in decadent Berlin. They went to Dax's favorite beer halls, getting stuffed on bratwurst and sauerkraut. Anna playfully mentioned that her people had actually invented sauerkraut and that his people had stolen the recipe.

"Anna, my love, I love bratwurst almost as much as my Chinese lover, but sauerkraut is crap. Your people can have it back." joked Dax as they feasted and drank great quantities of German beer.

They topped off the joyous evening with a visit to one of the infamous hedonistic nightclubs Berlin was famous for. Anna was quite startled when Dax pointed out that some of the pretty fräuleins that flirted with the customers were, in fact, men in drag. It was the first time Anna was aware that there were men who found sexual pleasure in dressing up as women. Though they could not afford it, Anna and Dax ordered expensive shots of cognac.

"Dax, my horny little friend," said a tall, pale-faced man with slicked-back blond hair. "I thought you were going to 'Gagaland' to become a famous star. What happened to the dream, old friend?"

"I suppose my salami was too large for the tastes of American fräuleins," laughed Dax with gusto. "Otto, dear friend! We were such good friends before I left Germany."

Otto interrupted, "Since we were children. The world has changed so much, but our friendship will never change. Not six thousand miles or three years will change it."

"My dear Otto, please allow me to introduce you to my lady friend and fellow actor, Anna May Wong," voiced Dax proudly.

Otto grinned slightly and shook Anna's hand in a perfunctory manner. "Fräulein Wong, I wish to speak to my friend Dax in private for a moment," he spoke abruptly, then pulled Dax away to a quiet corner.

It was obvious to Anna that Dax's friend was not overjoyed to see his old friend with a Chinese lover. She watched the two men speak rather heatedly in their native German language. She was curious about what the odd symbol represented on Otto's armband.

The heated conversation ended when Otto stormed away. Dax returned to sit with Anna, his face etched with pain. When he sat down beside her, his demeanor suddenly returned to a jovial mood.

"What is wrong, Dax?"

Dax smiled widely to lighten the dark mood. "Oh, do not worry your lovely head over Otto's rude behavior. My old friend does not approve of me sharing a bed with a person who is not of the Aryan race."

"What the hell is Aryan, Dax? And what does that silly design on his armband mean?"

Dax took a long gulp of beer, reluctant to reply. He then nervously lit a cigarette.

"Dax, the answer must not be good if you need a drink and a cigarette to calm yourself before answering."

"Anna, my love, Otto is a member of the emerging Nazi political party, an Aryan is a member of the superior Caucasian race. Otto has explained to me that it is blasphemy to taint my pure blood by bedding a lowly Mongoloid. The symbol you see on Otto's armband is called a *swastika;* it represents the Nazi party and the pure Aryan race."

Anna's mind began to spin with mixed emotions. "And what now? Do you plan to leave your yellowed-skinned girlfriend because your old friend Otto wills it?" she snapped.

"Of course not. You are my girl and I am your man. No racist, hate-mongering bastard is going to tell me different, even if he is a longtime friend." Dax kissed her with genuine affection. "Forget about Otto and the Nazis. We have more important things to deal with; namely, both of our brilliant future careers in European films."

15

For the next few weeks, Ana rehearsed for endless hours with the other principal actors in Eichberg's upcoming film. When the actual film production began, Anna was immediately beaten down by the demanding German director. During each day of filming, Eichberg would browbeat Anna and the other actors and crew, from the first minute until the final moments of the day's shoot. Unaccustomed to such taskmaster directors back in America, Anna would arrive home at her flat each evening trembling and often crying from the stressful day.

In the beginning, Dax would be there with open arms and a hot cup of tea to greet Anna. To relieve her anxiety, he would remove her shoes and sensually massage her feet. She took some solace in the fact that a handsome, caring man was there to dote over her and provide comforting words.

But one evening, after returning from the film shoot, Anna was troubled to see that Dax was not there at the door to greet her. On the kitchen table was a note stating that he had gone out with friends for a few hours of beer drinking, Anna was perplexed as to whether her lover had simply gone out for a few beers with male friends, or had he found another lover? Was Dax growing bored with her? She thought that Dax had seemed less amicable the last few weeks. They had not made love in a long time and he seemed to be preoccupied with something.

"Dax is perhaps despondent because his friend Herr Eichberg gave me work and did not offer him anything, even though they are friends," said Anna under her breath.

She sat up waiting for Dax's return, despite her need to rise early the next day. It was three in the morning when Dax came stumbling in. He had clearly been drinking and was rambling something in German.

"Anna, darling, you should not be up. You need your beauty sleep to make your big picture with Herr Richard."

Anna heated a cup of coffee for him. "Dax, my love, what is wrong? Are you no longer happy with me? Is there another woman?" asked Anna flat out.

He chuckled meekly. "Girlfriend, there is no one else. Every man is entitled to an occasional night of fellowship with his male friends," responded Dax glibly as he retired to bed without further explanation for being out so late.

Anna didn't know what to make of his odd behavior. She was deeply concerned, but as much as she loved him, the completion of her movie had to be her main priority for the time being.

For the next several weeks, the couple hardly spoke to one another. Their relationship was weakening. It did not matter. Anna was working fifteen-hour days and returning home each night exhausted. She no longer noticed Dax's frequent absences or cared about it.

When the grueling film was finally completed, a gala premiere was held in Berlin. Both the director and the film's actors, which included Anna, received a standing ovation after the film's screening. At the party held after the premiere, Anna was congratulated by countless new fans. A striking, tall blond woman spontaneously kissed her on the lips. "Fräulein Wong, your glory precedes you. Germany loves you, but like a full-length raccoon coat, you may be only a passing fad. In any case, I wish you good luck, providing your shadow is not longer than mine." Her voice carried a slight lisp. She planted another kiss on Anna's lips, then walked away.

Anna was quite stunned by the strange woman's forwardness, and stood there, speechless.

Eichberg approached her, laughing and clapping mockingly. "Fräulein Anna, welcome to German movies,"

"Herr Richard, who was that woman?" asked Anna.

"Anna, that memorable woman is Germany's most beloved and famous film actress, Marlene Dietrich. Count yourself lucky. Marlene is usually not so kind to her competition."

Anna giggled. "Richard, I do not think a lowly Chinese girl would give a beautiful blond gwah lo actress much competition," she stated, more amused by the eccentric woman than offended.

"Where is your handsome gentleman friend Dax?" asked Richard.

"Dax wishes he could be here for this momentous occasion, but regrettably, he is ill with the stomach flu."

In truth, Dax could not attend because he was in a state of drunkenness.

"A pity," Eichberg replied. "I hope Dax recovers soon. In any case, on a different subject, no doubt you think I am an asshole slave driver, as do most actors who work under me."

Anna was going to politely disagree, even though she did think so, as did many after experiencing his demanding style of directing. But Eichberg interjected before she could respond.

"Of course, you agree I am an asshole, but you are too kind to admit it. But hear me out, dear lady. Tomorrow you will read in the German newspapers nothing but glowing praise over your masterful performance in *Song*. If I had not been the hard-driving prick that I was, your performance would have been as memorable and as moving as watered-down beer."

Anna laughed hysterically. "Herr Richard, I do not think I will ever understand Germans, but if you wish to beat me with a club, so be it—as long as the critics and the German people love me," she exclaimed as they hugged each other.

True to Eichberg's prediction, film critics praised Anna's European debut with such complimentary words as "a subtle, masterful performance," "electrifying," and "a moving performance." German audiences became enchanted with the Chinese-American actress. During the following year, Eichberg directed her in another popular, high-grossing film titled *The City Butterfly*. Like the Phoenix, Anna had risen from the ashes, and with her renewed success she was able to move from her modest one-room flat to a luxury penthouse located in an upper-class section of Berlin. Despite the growing rift between her and Dax, she permitted him to live with her in the new residence, partly out of gratitude for helping her obtain work, and with the hope that she could rekindle a relationship with the man she still loved deeply.

Undoubtedly, Dax's growing distance and temperamental outbursts were due to his jealousy over her success and his failure to renew his own sagging film career. But Anna sensed that an underlying issue was causing the problems in their relationship.

Despondent, she walked for long hours as she waited for the beginning of rehearsals for her fourth German movie. She took comfort in being noticed by excited German fans, who stopped her on the streets and requested autographs, expressing their joy and the inspiration they got from viewing her movies. It felt so refreshing to once again have giddy fans praising her work and asking for her autograph. The welcome attention helped her to forget the growing distance between her and her lover.

All of this was erased during one of her walks. Anna was shocked to see men in brown shirts picketing a movie theater that was showing one of her movies. Creeping closer to get a better look, she recognized the swastika armbands on their arms.

That is the same armband Otto was wearing the night we saw him at the bar, she thought. Frustrated, she yelled, "What do you want?"

One protester, who spoke English, approached Anna and spat on her. "Germany is an exclusive country where only the pure Aryan race is allowed to live," he growled. "We have no room here for Jews, niggers, or chinks. If you are the actress Fräulein Wong, go back to where you came from. You are polluting my people with poisonous, decadent thoughts."

Anna could not believe the man's caustic words. "Sir, you are not the first person to spit on me and perhaps won't the last, but you are not worthy of my attention," she snapped and attempted to walk away.

The Nazi grabbed her arm, forcefully spinning her around. Two burly men came to Anna's aid, one knocking the offending man down while his partner kicked another protester in the groin. Sporting a bloody nose, the fallen man was assisted up by his comrades. The Nazi protesters cursed Anna and her rescuers in German. Shaking their fists, they slowly backed away.

"My apologies, Fräulein Wong. Those Nazi thugs do not represent all of Germany," said one of the men who had come to her rescue.

"Sadly, the Nazi political party is rising in Germany. Germany is in a deep depression. A starving man would vote for the devil if he thought he could put food in his belly," spoke the other rescuer.

An elderly woman wiped the spit off Anna's face with her handkerchief. "A Nazi monster is a candidate for the chancellor of Germany—a monster named Adolf Hitler. I pray to God that the Nazis will not destroy my country. We love you, Fräulein Wong. Do not let those bullies get you down."

On a notepad, Anna wrote out autographs to the two men and the woman who had helped her. "I am indebted to you kind people," she proclaimed.

Shaken but unhurt, she returned to her flat. Dax was sitting slumped in a chair, an empty bottle of schnapps at his feet. Staring blankly, he seemed indifferent that Anna had returned from her walk.

"Dax, a horrible thing happened to me while I was on my walk. I saw men picketing a movie theater where *The City Butterfly* was showing it. It was so frightening. Those bastards tried to attack me and one son-of-a-bitch spit on me. I could have been beaten badly by those sons-of-bitches if a couple of good men hadn't come to my rescue. Those monsters were wearing those Nazi symbols on their arms, like the one your friend Otto was wearing."

Dax shrugged his shoulders. "Anna, my love, how dare those gentlemen offend you. Do they not know the great Anna May Wong is a major film star back in America, and is soon to be one in Germany?" he snapped. He rose and planted a slobbery kiss on Anna's lips. "At least, my love, you were noticed. Would anyone give a shit if Dax Dortmunder dropped dead on a city street?"

Anna's eyes began to well up as she wrapped her arms around Dax tightly. "My beloved man, is that why you have built a wall between us these last few weeks? Because I have steady work acting in movies and you do not? Please be patient, my dear man. You're handsome and talented. Just give it a little time."

"A little time? How much is 'a little time'...a hundred years?" shouted Dax. "I am going out. Do not wait up for me."

"Is there another woman? Please don't leave, Dax. Let me make some coffee and we will sort this mess out," Anna pleaded as she grasped his arm to hold him back.

Dax violently pushed her against the wall, then stormed out the door. Dazed, Anna struggled to regain her composure as she staggered to the window just in time to see Dax board a streetcar.

She sat on the floor battling her emotions. She asked herself the same question over and over: Did she really love Dax or did she pretend to love him out of fear of being alone? She laughed in self-examination. Like many women and men of color, she knew that to have a gwah lo lover was an ego-building elixir that made them feel equal—or perhaps superior—to the gwah lo. She opened up her own bottle of whiskey, which she kept hidden under the mattress. Pulling the cork, she took a swig of the liquor.

She noticed a slip of paper on the floor lying beside the empty schnapps bottle. Written on the paper was the address to a public square.

Is he going there to rendezvous with another woman? I must find out what the future holds for me, reflected Anna, and left her apartment.

Upon arriving at the public square, she was greeted by a massive crowd—thousands of people who were applauding and screaming, "Hail Hitler!" Off in the distance stood a man with a comical-looking Charlie Chaplin mustache. He was giving an emotional, engrossing speech. Anna recognized Hitler immediately. She had seen his face in the newspapers.

The rabid crowd roared in approval after every sentence of Hitler's fervent speech. Standing beside him were a number of his loyal followers. Squinting her eyes, Anna was shocked to see Dax standing on the platform with the crazed speaker.

Bravely, Anna fought her way to the speaker's platform. Due to the dim light and the crowd's hypnotic attention toward the speaker, no one noticed the that the woman pushing her way toward the platform was not white.

After much pushing and shoving, Anna reached the stage. She shouted out Dax's name, but her voice was lost to the din of the raucous crowd. He didn't see her attempts to gain his attention by waving at him. Anna was desperate. She pulled a fistful of change from her coat pocket and threw it at Dax. With coins pelting him, Dax at last noticed Anna standing below him.

"Anna, why are you here?" he shouted as he assisted her to the stage.

"Why are *you* here?" she replied sharply.

Before Dax could answer, the other men on the stage noticed Anna's Asian features.

"Dax, you son-of-a-bitch traitor. You said you were leaving your chink whore!" cried one man.

Hitler himself noticed Anna standing a few feet from him. He pointed a menacing finger toward her, then spoke to the crowd. "My fellow Germans, this is part of our struggle, to rid the Fatherland of inferior people like this!"

One of the men standing near Hitler was one of the picketers who had assaulted Anna at the movie theater. Recognizing her, he whispered something in Hitler's ear. Hitler looked at her with narrowed eyes.

"My fellow countrymen and women, I have just been informed that this Asian bitch is the movie actress Anna May Wong. Like the Jews, she is destroying our beloved Fatherland." Hitler's voice seemed to grow louder and more intense with each word. "This yellow whore is corrupting the minds and souls of our German youth with her soft-yellow skin and exotic, narrow eyes. Fräulein Wong is tainting the blood of our Aryan young men with inferior Mongoloid blood."

Fearing for her safety, Dax told Anna to run. Anna did not want to give Hitler and his party the satisfaction of showing fear and running away. But Hitler's men grabbed her arms, preventing her from fleeing even had she wanted to.

"My fellow countrymen and women, what should we do with inferiors who want to undermine the new Third Reich, which I promise will last a thousand years?" screeched Hitler.

"Kill her! Kill her!" cried thousands of voices.

With a demonic grin, Hitler whispered to one of his underlings, "Teach Fräulein Wong a proper German lesson, but do not kill her. We do not need a martyr."

As Anna struggled to free herself from Hitler's subordinates, one man struck her in the face, which marked only the beginning of a savage beating. With each blow, the frenzied crowd applauded with glee. Like crazed, mad dogs, the Nazi men tore off her clothes as they continued to punch and kick her face and body. Strangely, Dax made no attempt whatsoever to stop the horrific attack. Instead, he cowered at the back of the stage, burying his face in his hands and sobbing.

Mercifully, Anna lost consciousness.

16

itler laughed insanely, as if watching some form of entertainment as the beating continued. The crowd erupted in applause and chants of, "Drive her out!" Luckily, before she could sustain further injuries, the police came to Anna's rescue after passersby reported the incident.

A few suspects were arrested, but Hitler was above reproach given his high political status.

One police officer kindly covered Anna's battered, naked body with his coat and carried her off the stage to await the arrival of an ambulance.

The following morning, Anna awoke in a German hospital with her head heavily bandaged. As her eyes came into focus, she saw Dax standing over her, holding her hand.

"My darling Anna, thank God you were not killed."

She abruptly pulled her hand away from his grasp. "You lying bastard! You said it didn't matter that your Nazi friends did not want you to have a chink girlfriend. What kind of man would stand by and do absolutely nothing to stop his woman from being beaten into unconsciousness? I never want to see you again!"

Dax began to cry, "My sweet Anna, I love you and always will, but you do not understand. The Nazis will soon have total power over Germany. Hitler and his thugs are ruthless. The bastard has twenty bodyguards. I am only one man. It is so much easier being the hero in a movie. My family owns several businesses in Berlin and they have—*we* have—much to lose if we do not kiss the Nazis' asses."

Anna glared at him. "And what of the sons-of-bitches that beat me and left me naked? Will you at least testify against them?"

Dax laughed painfully. "Dear, you have not been listening to what I told you. The Nazis are Germany's new taskmasters and Hitler is their god. Those bastards who beat you were jailed for perhaps an hour, then fined five marks each, the equivalent of about one American dollar."

Anna grabbed a pitcher of water that sat on a portable table and tossed the water at Dax. He was dripping wet and felt deep guilt.

"I am so sorry for all the pain the Nazis caused you—that I caused you. Good-bye, Anna."

Anna looked away as he departed. Then she let out a bitter giggle, fighting through the pain. "My German lover sold his soul to the devil. I hope the two of them will be very happy together."

A nurse entered with a breakfast tray, which Anna declined. She informed the nurse that all she needed was a cigarette. Although her jaw, along with most of the rest of her body, was painful, Anna didn't care. She insisted that the nurse place the cigarette in her mouth and light it. After doing as she was told, Anna ordered the nurse to leave.

Puffing on a cigarette seemed to be her only respite after her terrible ordeal. She struggled to sit up to gaze out the window. "Dax was right, Berlin is a very beautiful city," she whispered. She smiled, reflecting on the irony of her life decisions. *I left the Gold Mountain to rekindle my career, but also to escape the hateful racism in America, only to be nearly beaten to death by the German Nazis, who seem to hate everybody who doesn't have blue eyes and skin the color of toothpaste,* she thought ruefully.

A soft knock on the door interrupted her thoughts.

"Whoever is there, go. I do not need anyone to hold my hand!" shouted Anna.

The door slowly opened to reveal the director, Richard Eichberg. "Fräulein Anna, you are too sexy for me to just want to hold your hand," he joked as he entered with a bouquet of red roses.

"Richard, look at me. I am no longer sexy."

Eichberg kissed Anna on her lips.

"Ouch!" she cried.

"Sorry, your lips must be sore along with most everything else. Don't worry. The beautiful woman I once knew will return once your wounds heal." Eichberg set a chair beside her and drew out a flask of fine cognac, placing a small portion in two glasses. He handed one glass to Anna.

"All the medicine I will need today," quipped Anna as the two of them clicked glasses in a toast. "Richard," she continued. "Your fellow Germans gave me a warm reception. I am used to such a cordial greeting. The police on the Gold Mountain also gifted me a visit to the hospital, but that was my own doing. Welcome to Germany." Anna laughed, fighting back the pain.

Richard shook his head. "Oh, my darling Anna, I heard about your beating back in America, but please do not blame the German people for the actions of a few hate mongers. The fact that the three movies you were in under my brilliant direction grossed over five million marks is proof of Germany's love for you. It is the new political party, the Nazis, that is about to take the reins of the government that despise not just you, but the Jews and all people of color. This brings me to the reason for my visit. I did not come here just to wish you well. Germany is no longer safe for you, and as much as I love you, Fräulein Anna, I regret that we can no longer make wonderful movies together." Eichberg handed Anna an envelope. "My dear friend, in this envelope is a ticket to Paris and an address to a Fräulein Adrian Courtland. She is a fellow American expatriate. She is of negro extraction and will assist you in your relocation to France. Plus, I have enclosed the name and address of a colleague—a film director who will give you work. The French make inferior movies compared to the Germans, but the French, like the Germans, will love you. You picked up the German language rather easily, so you should have no problem picking up the French language."

For a few moments, Anna gazed at the envelope, then tossed it on the floor.

"Richard, my beloved friend and mentor, in America the gwah lo, which is an unflattering term for whites, spat on me. The sons-of-bitches would only give me roles where I was a stereotypical yellow whore. I ran to Europe to escape those humiliations. I will run no more."

Eichberg picked up the envelope and placed it on her lap. "Anna, I love you as much as my own children. You have suffered back in your native California, only to suffer more in my country. You are a strong and brave woman. You had to be, in order to survive, but the Nazi devils are more ruthless than anyone you have ever met. I have Jewish friends whose lives I fear for. There are rumors that the Nazis, when they gain power, will round up the two million Jews living in Germany and send them to prison camps and kill them all. With that much irrational hate, they will have no qualms about killing Chinese people as well."

Anna swallowed the remainder of cognac in her glass and began to giggle absurdly. "Richard, my friend, you really believe the Nazis would kill me, plus millions of Jews? Would that not be a very drastic solution?"

Richard poured another measure of cognac into their glasses. "I have listened to Adolf Hitler on the radio. The man is insane. Once he is elected chancellor of Germany, there will be no stopping him and his Nazi party. Perhaps I am wrong about them committing mass murder, but do you want to put your life on the line to prove me wrong?" Richard took her hand and kissed it softly. "I beg you to go to Paris. You have a powerful voice. You cannot change the world buried in a six-foot-deep hole."

Anna swallowed the second glass of cognac in a single gulp. With a hand mirror, she gazed at her swollen, bruised face. "I was beaten and stripped naked by those cowardly sons-of-bitches. Once they are in power, maybe they will take my head the next time." She smiled at Richard. "I suppose I will have to learn to like eating food with heavy sauces," she joked.

Richard kissed Anna gently on the cheek, trying not to cause her more pain in the process. "You set German films on fire. Now you will do the same in France. May God watch over and protect you, my cherished friend. If you do not believe in the gwah lo God, then I hope whatever god you believe in will watch over you."

After only a few days of recuperation, against her doctor's wishes, Anna packed her things and prepared to board a train bound for Paris, France. While riding in a taxi to the train station, she witnessed numerous businesses that had been vandalized with hateful graffiti degrading the Jews.

"Perhaps Richard is right. The Nazis will stop at nothing to rid Germany of anyone who is not pure white," spoke Anna under her breath as she rode through the streets of Berlin for the last time.

After arriving in Paris, she went directly to the address that Richard had given her.

Adrian Courtland...I have heard that name before, thought Anna as she walked the Bohemian east bank of the city searching for the residence.

After finally locating the woman's address, Anna hesitated to ring the doorbell. She was gripped with fear and knew that an uncertain future lay before her. Would she be up to whatever challenges she would encounter?

Anna slapped her face. *Get ahold of yourself, Anna May Wong. You already had the balls to start a new life in Germany; why should starting a new life in France be any different?* she said to herself in silent words.

Without further thought, she rang the doorbell. The door flung open, and there, standing before her, was a rather eccentric-looking black woman. She wore gaudy jewelry and her face was heavily made-up. Although it was midday, she wore a negligee and it appeared that she had just risen from bed.

With giddy exuberance, the woman wrapped her arms around

Anna. "Anna May Wong, from one expatriate to another, I welcome you to Paris. I am Adrian Courtland," she voiced before planting a sensual, wet kiss on Anna's lips.

As the black woman held her and kissed her, Anna realized that she had seen Courtland in the newspapers. She was an internationally famous dancer.

Servants of Indo-Chinese extraction carried Anna's luggage to her room. They spoke to her in their native tongue, and Anna looked at them with confusion.

Adrian cackled with amusement. "Anna darling, I forgot you are a person of a different color. You are of Chinaman persuasion and my servants are Indo-Chinaman."

Anna giggled, taking no offense. She knew Adrian was probably not aware that the term "Chinaman" was derogatory.

Once Anna was settled, Adrian invited her to a small snack of champagne and caviar. "Anna, Richard wrote me about those Nazi assholes taking over Germany. They hate Jews. And how do they feel about chinks and niggers?" she added sharply. "From the looks of your black-and-blue face and the bandages on your head, I would guess you already had a word or two with the sons-of-bitches before you left Germany."

Anna's demeanor suddenly turned morose with Adrian's comment. Adrian had touched a sensitive spot in her soul.

Adrian instructed one of her servants to bring something stronger to drink. The houseboy fetched a vintage bottle of whiskey and two shot glasses. As the servant began to pour a modest measure into each glass, Adrian snatched the bottle from him.

"Lao Chin, allow me to do the honors," she said as she filled each shot glass to the brim. Adrian clicked glasses with her newfound friend. "Down the hatch, girlfriend."

Both women emptied their glasses in a single gulp. Anna seemed a bit more at ease after the strong drink.

"Girlfriend, would it help to tell me what kind of shit you went through in Germany?"

Anna shook her head. "I do not think I will ever understand why the gwah los hate me. Gangsters called Nazis beat me severely, as you can see by my face. It was the second time that's happened to me. The first beating was at the hands of the gwah lo police back in California, all because a store owner would not let me buy a pretty dress I liked. But my beating in Germany I fear had much darker undertones. The Nazi bastards no doubt would have killed me were it not for my fame as a movie actress. I think that son-of-a-bitch Hitler, who looks like the comedian Charlie Chaplin, wants to murder every single soul in Germany who is not pure, pure white."

Adrian sat beside Anna, placing a comforting arm around her. "When you say 'gwah lo,' I am guessing you're talking about white folks. I like to call them 'peckerwoods.' In America, all men are created equal. That is unless you happen to be a nigger or a chink. They did a lot more than just beat my people. I had men relatives that were castrated, and they hung many of my black brothers from trees. A black sister wrote a song about that called 'Strange Fruit.' That is why I fled to France. The French treat me as their own, as they will you, my yellow sister." With that said, Adrian again kissed Anna on the lips, which Anna knew was more than just a friendly peck.

Anna pushed her any away. "What is wrong with us for the gwah lo to hate us so, Adrian?" she asked, hoping to draw attention away from Adrian's advances, but also because she genuinely wanted her opinion.

Adrian took two cigarettes out of a gold case that was resting on the coffee table. "You smoke?"

Before Anna could answer, Adrian shoved a cigarette in Anna's mouth and lit it. She then placed the other cigarette in her own mouth and lit it. Smoking a cigarette gave Adrian a moment to contemplate Anna's question.

"My yellow friend, in my opinion, the peckerwoods that beat, rape, and kill us are frightened little boys afraid of the dark. I think they hate themselves more than they hate us. It's only when they have someone to look down on that they feel good about themselves." She took hold of Anna's hand. "What a bullshit, hard world we live in, Mademoiselle Wong. The only advice I have is don't let the goddamn peckerwoods, or anyone else, run your life or hurt you. The gwah lo devils knocked us both down, but we're only defeated if we don't get back up." She grinned widely.

After listening to Adrian's reassuring words, for the first time in a long while, Anna felt a calm sense of well-being. She gazed at Adrian enigmatically. Aside from Auntie Lilly's chauffeur, Adrian was the only other hak gwai she had ever known. She immediately felt a bond with Adrian. She felt deep shame for having reservations about living with a hak gwai after Richard had informed her of Adrian's race. Subconsciously, she too was that frightened little boy looking down on someone of a different race to feel good herself.

This time it was Anna who made the advances. She kissed Adrian with as much affection as when she and Dax had been lovers. Anna had never felt an attraction to a woman before, but the mounting issues, such as severing her relationship with Dax, her assault, and her sudden relocation to a foreign nation, had left her feeling no familiarity with anything. It weighed heavily on her fragile state.

For the remainder of the day, Adrian gave Anna a grand tour of her beloved city. She delighted in taking her to a café, where Adrian introduced Anna to other fellow American expatriates Ernest Hemingway and F. Scott Fitzgerald.

Adrian's zest for living the good life was beginning to rub off on Anna. It caused her to reminisce about her joyous times making her first film with Douglas Fairbanks, and her bittersweet times with Aunt Lilly and Cilla.

That evening, Adrian prepared a cheese soufflé complimented by a vintage red wine. Afterwards, they drank more whiskey, talking and laughing as if they had been friends for a lifetime. Adrian taught Anna the tango, which was the new dance craze in Paris.

As they danced with their bodies pressed against each other, Anna forgot, if only for the moment, the ugliness she had left behind in Berlin.

Finally, after a long day and a night of reveling, the two women collapsed, embracing each other on Adrian's huge bed.

17

In the morning around nine the women were rudely awakened by the phone ringing. Badly hungover, Adrian answered the phone in slurred words. On the other end of the line she could hear loud laughter.

"Adrian, my sweet, from the sound of your voice you had one too many glasses of the bubbly last night," quipped the caller.

"Who the hell is disturbing me at this ridiculous hour?" Adrian shouted into the phone. She heard more laughter.

"Adrian dear, I am deeply pained that you did not recognize your old friend Jean Michel Beaufait, France's greatest film director. My colleague in Germany has sent word to me that his protégé, a Mademoiselle Wong, has come to Paris and I am to give her work. Herr Eichberg also mentioned that she would be staying at your residence. I do hope you did not corrupt her too much," joked Beaufait.

"Shit!" spoke Adrian under her breath. "Uh...Anna is a bit indisposed. She will need a little freshening up."

"In other words, you got the poor woman drunk on her first day in Paris. No matter. Tell Mademoiselle Wong to come to my office at Diamond Studios after you get some strong coffee down her."

Adrian grimaced at the director's request to see Anna on such short notice "But...but Jean—"

The director abruptly hung up the phone before she could explain that, given her injuries and being as hungover as she was, Anna would be in no condition to see an important film director.

Frantically, Adrian awakened Anna, who was groggy and had a

splitting headache.

Anna spoke with a slurred voice. "Adrian, please let me go back to sleep. My head is killing me."

Adrian shook her fiercely, then shouted to one of the servants to bring a pot of hot coffee. "Girlfriend, get ahold of yourself. Your destiny called, his name is Jean Michel Beaufait. He's the most significant film director in all of France. His Majesty is requesting an audience with you. This might be your last chance to grab the brass ring. A peckerwood can have more than one chance, but us yellow and black niggers usually just get one."

Adrian poured hot coffee down Anna's throat while a female servant fished through Anna's luggage searching for an appropriate dress.

"No, not that one! No, damn it, not that one!" screeched Adrian as she critiqued each dress the maid held up before her.

As Anna's head began to clear, she stood naked in front of a full-length mirror. She became quite exasperated as she viewed her battered face and body. "Damn. A pile of horse dung is prettier than I am," she exclaimed.

Adrian was losing patience. "Girlfriend, Monsieur Beaufait wants to see you now! Not two weeks from now when your bruises will be mostly gone. I am the Picasso of women's make-up. When I am finished with your face, Marlene Dietrich will be jealous."

Anna giggled at Adrian's statement. "Marlene Dietrich is *already* jealous," she remarked, having already met Dietrich in Germany.

"'Nothing works. Sue Lyn, fetch my marvelous yellow dress— the one I wore when I had an audience with the president of Italy," Adrian ordered.

Placing Anna at a make-up table, Adrian meticulously applied make-up to Anna's face. "What do you think, girlfriend?" she asked when she was finished.

Anna laughed. "I resemble one of those streetwalkers I played so many times back in California."

To complete her transformation, Adrian planted a wide-brimmed hat on Anna's her head to cover her bandages. "Give 'em hell, Mademoiselle Wong," laughed Adrian. She started to kiss Anna on the lips, then pulled back so as not to smear her make-up.

A short time later, while riding in the taxi to Beaufait's office, Anna nervously mumbled what she might say to impress the man.

The taxi driver adjusted his rearview mirror to get a better look at his passenger. "Madame, you look very familiar. May I ask who are you?"

"Monsieur, do you watch movies?" she replied.

"Oui! Oui! *The Red Lantern* and *Toll of the Sea*. You are the American actress Anna May Wong. We French love American cinema."

For the remainder of the ride, the driver and Anna carried on a pleasant conversation about the good and bad aspects of American and European films.

Upon arriving at the film studio, the taxi driver refused to be paid. "Madame Wong I will accept no pay. It is the least I can do for all the beauty you have brought to the world at a time when it is in great need of it."

Anna placed a kiss on both of the driver's cheeks. "Merci, mon ami," she said. She had picked up a little French from Adrian.

With a bit of apprehension, Anna was poised to knock on the director's office door when she heard a voice on the other side.

"Enter, Mademoiselle Wong."

Upon entering, Anna saw a dashing, middle-aged man sitting behind his desk, wearing an expensive, tailored, blue blazer. He had a thin mustache and piercing blue eyes.

"Please, take a seat, Mademoiselle Wong."

For a short time, Beaufait said nothing as he continued to gaze strangely at Anna, he then burst out in laughter. "Mademoiselle, do you plan on joining the circus? You are as heavily made-up as a circus clown and the brim of your hat is as big as a beach umbrella."

"My apologies, Monsieur Beaufait," Anna said. "You see—"

The man interrupted before the embarrassed Anna could complete her explanation. "Anna, mon ami, you need not explain. My colleague Richard Eichberg has already notified me of your injuries sustained by those Nazi thugs. It is my guess that the big hat is to hide your bandaged head."

Beaufait poured Anna and himself some thirty-year-old cognac.

"Anna, my love, we have been friends for perhaps three minutes and thirty seconds," stated Beaufait, gazing at his watch. "But I have known you longer. I have followed your career over the last few years and have watched both your American films and the ones my German colleague, Richard Eichberg, directed you in. You have a most excellent screen presence. You need not audition for me. You have been doing so for the last four or five years in the movies you've been in. Together, we will make history." He smiled. "Take this script. The name of the character is Hai-tang. You play a Chinese dancer who falls in love with a Russian military officer. Your relationship with him becomes complicated when his superior officer also has eyes for you. Study your role carefully. We begin rehearsals two weeks from today. Try not to party too much with my party girlfriend Adrian." Beaufait handed her the script and chuckled.

Ignoring the pain from her injuries, Anna stood and embraced the director. "Oh, Mr. Beaufait, thank you a million times for saving my life."

"Anna, call me Jean Michel. When *L'Amour Maitre des Choses* is released, the French audiences will fall in love with you, and someday, so will the entire world. Now, go and study your ass off." Beaufait grinned widely.

After returning to Adrian's home with giddy enthusiasm, Anna asked Adrian to help her study the plot and the lead female role she was to play. The two women drank a toast of champagne in celebration.

"In France, there is no Myrna Loy to steal my thunder," remarked Anna as she and Adrian swore a pact that it would be their last binge of strong spirits until the completion of Anna's movie.

Like Lillian Gish before her, Adrian would assist Anna almost every waking hour, when she was not performing in her dance revues at Parisian music halls. She pretended to be the lead male as well as having long conversations regarding the personality and tone of each sentence of dialogue Anna's character would speak.

The director was greatly impressed with Anna's preparedness on the first day of rehearsal. A couple of days into the rehearsal, Anna was surprised and delighted to see her German mentor, Richard Eichberg, sitting on the stage when she came for the day's practice.

"Fräulein Anna, you have not yet rid yourself of your slave-driving director just yet," he teased. "My good friend Herr Jean Michel has kindly given me the director's job for your first French endeavor. No one knows and understands the quirks and nuances of Anna May Wong as well as I do."

They embraced fondly.

Having worked with Eichberg in three of his films in Germany, the director and actress made a fine team.

As Anna had hoped, *L'Amour Maitre des Choses* was a rousing success that led to other popular French films she starred in. Soon the British film industry caught wind of this unique Asian actress who enchanted the French audiences, and she received offers to act in British films as well. Anna began to commute between Paris and London. The first British film, titled *The Flame of Love*, was an English version of *L'Amour Maitre des Choses*.

Anna was now riding the crest of a profession many sought but few—especially non-whites—succeeded at.

She heard word that her former lover and collaborator, Sessue Hayakawa, was residing in London. Hayakawa had informed her that he too was relocating to Europe when they were still in California, but gave no specifics as to what country. When Anna attempted to contact him, he did not respond. She thought he was too embarrassed that he hadn't gained the success she had. Anna made no further effort to contact him, knowing that his fierce pride would shame him.

The Chinese-American actress was now insanely happy and at peace with herself. Aside from adoring fans and a substantial income, Anna found a true kindred soul in Adrian. They were both of a minority race and both had been born and raised in a prejudiced, white-dominated America.

Anna frequented visits to the *Folies Le Grande* to watch Adrian in her famous black revue. In some routines she would dance nude, much to the delight of her loyal audience. Having equal fame and adoration, Anna would sign hundreds of autographs before the start of each show. It was an idyllic life for Anna, but on some days, especially at the end of a long drinking binge with Adrian, Anna would reflect on the haunting words Sessue had once told her—that fame and riches were not lasting. She knew the man's words rang true. She had fallen out of favor in Hollywood due, in part, to her own refusal to continue playing stereotyped roles when more important roles went to gwah lo women made-up to look Asian. Then, in Germany, where her career was beginning to rekindle, she had been forced out by the rising Nazis, who did not tolerate anyone not of pure white blood. Now she was the darling of France and England.

"This too will end one day," she mouthed under her breath as she and Adrian sat drinking cognac and listening to a phonograph playing Mozart chamber music.

"What did you say, my love?" asked Adrian.

"Nothing of importance. You did say coloreds only have one chance to grab the brass ring. I fell off the Gold Mountain twice, and here I am in Paris, sitting atop that glittering mountain once again."

Adrian giggled and kissed Anna. "All right, girlfriend. I was wrong. Beautiful Chinese girls get a few more chances, but my point is that for yellow or black niggers, the brass ring is so much farther away than it is for peckerwoods."

18

In 1932, the German general election was less than a year away. It was obvious that the Nazis were poised to take control of Germany. Almost daily, Anna read in Paris newspapers about the Nazi's persecution of the Jews and other groups not considered by the Nazis to be of the Aryan race. Anna knew, as did most people in Europe, that the Nazis would not be satisfied with simply controlling Germany. Certainly, the madman Hitler would not be satisfied until his regime ruled the entire continent of Europe, if not the world. She was deeply concerned about her fate, and Adrian's.

It was early one morning, and Anna sat in Adrian's garden, which resembled a painting by Renoir. Adrian, not being an early riser, was still in bed. Anna sat under a shady willow tree, watching goldfish move in and out from under lily pads in the garden pond. A maid brought Anna her morning coffee. On the coffee tray was a letter addressed to her. The return address was Paramount Studios, Hollywood, California.

Eagerly, Anna tore open the envelope. The sender was the president of Paramount Studios. He wrote that his people had been closely monitoring her burgeoning career in Europe, and he was inviting her back into the fold. He went on to say the only really good movies made in the world were Hollywood movies, and that she was wasting her career with artsy French or boring English movies. Anna cackled loudly. He was mirroring what Herr Eichberg had told her—that Germany made the best movies in the world. He then gave a warning that she had already considered—that there was growing tension in Europe and, should the Nazis take control of

France or Great Britain, not only would her career be in jeopardy, but her life could also be in danger. And lastly, he stated that America would welcome her back home with open arms.

Anna tossed the letter back onto the tray. "The hell with him," she spat. "The Gold Mountain was never my home. The gwah los never made me and my Chinese brothers and sisters feel that America was our home, even though many of us were born on the Gold Mountain." She tore up the letter and tossed the shreds on the ground.

Anna said nothing to Adrian about the Paramount letter, or to anyone else. She went to England to complete yet another film. Upon her return, at Adrian's suggestion, they vacationed on the Mediterranean coast in the South of France, famously known as the Riviera. They romped in the bath-warm waters of the turquoise sea, then sat under a large beach umbrella drinking wine.

"On a clear day, you can see Africa from here," spoke Adrian in jest.

"What sharp eyes you have, my love," replied Anna.

Adrian looked away. She had something to say to Anna, but was reluctant.

Anna noticed her hesitation. "Adrian, dear, you're usually not at a loss for words. I've known you long enough to know when something troubles you. Spit it out, girlfriend!"

"Very well," Adrian replied. She pulled out a beach bag and opened it to reveal a piece of paper held together with tape. It was the Paramount letter Anna had torn up and left in the garden. Adrian handed the letter to Anna.

"How did you get this?" she asked.

"Darling, no one tears a letter into a thousand pieces without good reason. I found it and told Lao Chin to tape the letter back to its original state. It took him several hours to accomplish it. Why didn't you tell me about the Paramount offer? It sounds like a great opportunity. You'll be a shining star in the heavens, just as you always wanted."

Anna placed her hand on Adrian's cheek. "I am already a bright star here in Europe. I am already living the good life with a beautiful partner. Why do you want me to go back to the Gold Mountain and leave everything I have worked so hard for here?"

Adrian rolled her eyes and grinned oddly. "My yellow bitch, the devil—or, if you prefer, the other name they go by, the Nazis—will soon have Germany by the family jewels. And they will not be satisfied till they have *everyone's* jewels. Have you heard of Hitler's chief filmmaker, Leni Riefenstahl?"

Anna nodded her head. "Of course I have. We met in Berlin. She has always treated me as a friend. I miss her."

"Friend my black ass. Leni only showed you one of her two faces. She may not be prejudiced against you or a negro dancing girl, but she has sold her soul to the devil. She is Hitler's puppet on a string. Just this very hour she is filming a movie which casts Jews, niggers, chinks—everyone except those self-lovin' snowflakes—as slobbering, decadent pigs. When those assholes take control of France, that is all everyone will see—Riefenstahl films that will make us look like retarded jungle apes, or films that make the Nazis look like goddamn gods. When that day comes, my China doll, your movie career will be in the shithouse. There is talk that the Nazis might put people like us in gas chambers. I believe Monsieur Eichberg already warned you that this might happen to you if you stay in Germany. Now I am warning you. This could happen in France. I beg you, my love, go back to America. Those peckerwoods might spit on you, but at least they won't make you worm food."

Anna was sobered by the pleading tone in Adrian's voice. She gazed out at the empty, calm sea, absorbing what Adrian had told her. "Adrian, my sweet love, you really want me to return to America? Once, when I was still making movies on the Gold Mountain, they sent me to Texas to promote one of my films. Everywhere we went there were two public restrooms; one labeled "colored only" and the other labeled "whites only." I was forced to use the "colored only" restrooms. This is the country you want me to live in?"

Adrian laughed. "Anna, my celestial lover, look at this face. Are you blind or just slow-witted? I am a colored woman. I had to piss in those same 'colored only' restrooms."

"Sorry, girlfriend," Anna said. "I was selfishly thinking only of myself. If you insist that I return to the Gold Mountain, then come with me."

Adrian lit a cigarette and began puffing nervously. "Hell no! Paris is my home. The French love me. And I love them. China girl, we are both so much alike. All our lives we have been fighting to fit in, to get that invitation to sit at the dinner table with those snooty peckerwoods, or gwah los, as you call them. You and I don't take no shit from whitey!" Adrian continued to puff on her cigarette. "I act like some crazy big-mouthed negro woman so I can get noticed. That is why the French love me so much. I am not afraid to speak my mind, instead of scrapin' and bowin', yes sir, thank you, sir. Back in America, I'm just a plain nigger."

Anna took the cigarette from Adrian's mouth, took a drag, then placed it back in her mouth. "Honey, we both know each other's pain, but you did say my life could be in danger if I stay in France. Wouldn't a negro woman also be risking her life in France if the Nazis come?"

"Anna, like you, I am nearly thirty. I've done more living in my short years than someone who is a hundred. I'm not afraid of dying. But you! You still have a lot of good movies to make. You need to give that uppity Myrna Loy some competition. Now, go back to America, goddamn it, and don't take no shit off them peckerwoods."

After returning to Paris, Anna attended Adrian's black revue at the *El Folies Le Grande* one last time. At the end of her revue, Adrian announced to the audience her special friend's return to America. The appreciative French gave her a standing ovation to show their fondness for the actress.

The mayor of Paris presented her with the key to the city. After informing Paramount of her intention to sign with their studio, a ticket on a chartered plane to America was sent to her by courier.

When the fateful day finally arrived for Anna's flight to the homeland she had left three years earlier, both she and Adrian were shocked to see thousands of French fans standing at the airport to bid Anna farewell. Anna kissed and hugged every person she could reach as she and Adrian waded through the crowd out to the tarmac. Before Anna stepped onto the plane, the two lovers and best friends giggled, never wanting to let go.

"There are no words left to say, girlfriend. We've said them already," voiced Anna as she and Adrian cried tears like a hard rain.

"Knock 'em dead, Anna May Wong!" shouted Adrian as Anna stepped onto the plane.

It was a long flight to New York City. Upon arrival, Anna immediately boarded a train, westward bound for Los Angeles. She was gripped with fear about her uncertain future—ironically, a fear more intense than when she had fled to Europe.

"Europe loved me, but on the Gold Mountain I was just a chink, a slant-eyed whore to the gwah los. Even my own people looked down on me for perpetuating the negative image of Chinese people. But the Chinese youth like me...." She shook her head and sighed. "Maybe the gwah los on the Gold Mountain have changed in three years."

19

Los Angeles has grown so much in my absence, thought Anna as she looked out the train window at the extensive construction and heavy traffic as she entered the city limits.

At the train station, a young gwah lo man dressed in a chauffeur's uniform approached Anna and warmly greeted her.

"Miss Wong, welcome home. The studio has a room reserved for you at the Beverly Hills Hotel. After you freshen up a tad, I will drive you to Paramount to meet the studio head and your director."

"How did you know who I was?" Anna asked.

The young man chuckled. "Miss Wong, I have been an enormous fan of yours for many years. I was only ten when I saw you in *The Toll of the Sea*. It was the first time I ever saw an Asian in a film. I have been in love with you from that day on."

Anna blushed with embarrassment as she got into the waiting limousine.

As they approached the iconic hotel, Anna thought about the name of the hotel, and recalled an incident that had occurred there when she was just starting out in the business.

"Young man, are you sure you are taking me to the right place? Years ago I was refused entrance to the Beverly Hills Hotel, even though I had an engraved invitation to attend a party there given by Douglas Fairbanks."

The chauffeur smiled. "Miss Wong, the same lo fon or gwah lo pricks, which I've heard is what your people call us, still run the Beverly Hills Hotel, but the head of Paramount Studios carries a lot of weight in Tinsel Town. For you, they have made an exception."

Once Anna had settled in at the hotel and refreshed herself, she was taken to Paramount Studios to meet the studio head and the director of her next film. When they pulled up to the studio entrance, an elderly security guard approached Anna.

"Miss Wong," he said. "You do not remember me. I am that son-of-a-bitch who bullied you years ago when you tried to get in the gate of the old Summit Studios. I lost my job over it." He offered a sheepish smile. "I deserved it. I beg your forgiveness. I didn't know I was picking on a future movie star." The old man looked away, seemingly too ashamed to look Anna directly in the eyes.

Anna stepped out of the limousine to hug the guard. "Sir, in those days we all had a lot of growing up to do. I forgive you, of course."

She returned to the limousine, and the chauffeur whisked her off to the office of the studio head. She felt overwhelmed by the enormity of the Paramount grounds. They were far larger than anything she had seen in Europe. Standing in front of the six-story offices of studio administration, she saw a distinguished-looking man dressed in a tailored suit surrounded by his subordinates.

"What an honor to at long last to meet the world's greatest female Asian actress, Anna May Wong. Please, allow me to introduce myself. I am Franklin Pritchard, head of Paramount Studios." He turned to an assistant who stood next to him, holding a bouquet of two-dozen red roses. "Blanche, the flowers please," he said, snapping his fingers.

Anna smiled as she accepted the flowers. "Mr. Pritchard, cut the bullshit. I am the world's greatest Asian female actress because no one else wanted the job."

For a moment, Pritchard and his staff stood speechless, stunned by the woman's outspoken candor. The studio head then erupted into outrageous laughter, followed by his subordinates.

"Miss Wong, you are an absolute delight. You're the only Chinese woman—or *any* woman, for that matter—who is not afraid to speak her mind. Please accompany me to my office. Your director is also looking forward to meeting the acid-tongued Anna May Wong."

Pritchard escorted Anna to his office, where she was greeted by a tall man who also sported an expensive tailored suit. "Anna, what a wonderful pleasure. My German countryman, Herr Eichberg, has told me so much about you. Please allow me to introduce myself. I am the humble director of your next blockbuster flicker, *Shanghai Express*. My name is Josef von Sternberg."

"Josef, Miss Wong is indeed a remarkable woman. She speaks fluently in your native tongue, German, and is also fluent in French, and has a passing knowledge of Yiddish and Italian. She can even speak with an English accent," exclaimed Pritchard.

"Mr. Pritchard, you did not include my own Chinese language," interjected Anna.

The two men laughed.

"Miss Wong," stated Pritchard, "you are an incredible, multi-talented young lady."

"Can you cook?" asked von Sternberg, half joking.

"*Ich tue*, but only delicious Cantonese-style foods," responded Anna, partially in German.

Both men applauded Anna's numerous talents. "Fräulein Anna, I believe this is the beginning of a beautiful relationship, both professionally and as good friends," declared Pritchard. "I believe your female co-star will fall in love with you as we have. No doubt you have heard of her—Marlene Dietrich, Germany's most cherished actress."

Anna flashed a forced smile, hiding her displeasure. "Of course. I would guess only a bushman in the Kalahari has not heard of God's gift to mankind," she sneered.

The men smiled politely, uncertain whether Anna's remark was a subtle, biting criticism of Dietrich or a genuine compliment.

"Uh, excellent, Miss Wong," Pritchard said. "Here is the script for *Shanghai Express*. Please meet Josef at six a.m., two weeks from today at stage 26A for the beginning of rehearsals. Welcome to

Paramount, Anna."

Pritchard hugged her warmly, which was followed by a hug from von Sternberg.

During the interlude before rehearsals, Anna paid a visit to her parents. After a three-year absence, the lifelong rift between them had lessened. Although Sam Sing and Lee You still disapproved of their daughter's unorthodox profession, they at long last accepted it and expressed their love toward their free-spirited daughter. After a couple days of feasting on fine Chinese food, which both daughter and mother prepared, Anna paid a visit to her mentor and beloved friend, Lillian Gish.

Gish was surprised and delighted. "The prodigal daughter returns! Welcome home!" joked Gish.

As when Anna was barely in her teens, Gish tutored her and rehearsed with Anna for her upcoming role in *Shanghai Express*.

On the first day of formal rehearsals at Paramount, Anna arrived promptly at the required time. She was cordially greeted by von Sternberg and other principal actors—the only exception being Marlene Dietrich. For two hours von Sternberg played her role of Shanghai Lily. Finally, Dietrich's personal guard swung open the door and held it for Dietrich. She waltzed in holding a cigarette on a long-stemmed holder.

"Herr Director, I am ready when you are to begin rehearsals," spoke Dietrich nonchalantly, giving no explanation or apology for her tardiness. She turned to Anna. "Ah, Fräulein Wong, we meet again. I hope you have studied your lines," added Dietrich, kissing Anna on both cheeks in a perfunctory manner.

For the next three weeks, the primary cast members rehearsed long, hard hours. Despite the fact that there was no love lost between the two illustrious actresses, they were both professionals and worked diligently to make their roles poignant, all under the direction of von Sternberg, who was regarded as one of cinema's greatest directors of women.

When the actual filming began, Anna was awed by the movie

set, which had been constructed to resemble a metropolitan city in China. Both Dietrich and Anna arrived on the set in the same limousine. Anna was welcomed with hearty applause by the film crew and the extras in remembrance of the entertaining movies she had made in Hollywood before her departure to Europe. Dietrich seethed with contemptuous jealousy, having received a less auspicious reception.

As the women sat on high canvas folding chairs waiting to begin their first scene together, Dietrich ranted in German to her assistant about the lack of acting talent her "cat-eating" fellow cast member possessed.

"Nein, Fräulein Marlene," sneered Anna. "I do not eat cats, and I can act circles around most German bitches."

Dietrich was in a state of shock. *"Sprechen sie Deutsch?"*

"Ja, I speak German fluently, as well as French and Chinese," replied Anna when Marlene asked her if she spoke German.

Dumfounded, Dietrich cursed under her breath in German as the make-up artist began to apply a few touch-ups to her face. She rudely slapped the make-up artist's hands away. "Enough!" she snapped, angered that her Chinese co-star knew she was mocking her. "I need no more make-up. Let's get this damn scene over with."

As the cameras were about to roll, von Sternberg explained to the women that in this particular scene the two characters are in a heated argument, culminating with Dietrich slapping Anna. Marlene grinned slyly when he informed her that she was supposed to slap Anna.

The women performed the moving scene beautifully, and when it came to the climactic part where Marlene was to slap Anna, she did so quite viciously. The slap was not make-believe or staged, and it caused Anna immediate, searing pain. Being a professional, Anna pushed through it and continued with the scene. She would not let Marlene have the satisfaction of knowing she had caused her any discomfort.

"Wunderbar!" exclaimed von Sternberg, quite pleased with the

scene. But being a perfectionist, he insisted on a retake.

Again, Dietrich harshly slapped Anna across the cheek, then grinned slyly at her.

Anna responded with her own subtle grin, then formed a fist and punched Dietrich in the face, causing her to fall on her back.

Crew members rushed to Marlene's aid, but she waved them away. "No! Stay back. We must finish the scene," she ordered.

She rubbed her painful jaw as a giggling Anna extended a hand to help her up. Marlene accepted, and as she rose off the floor, she struck Anna in the face with her other hand. Anna responded with another blow to Marlene's face. And so began an all-out melee as the two actresses exchanged blows, one after another. Dietrich began swearing at Anna in German, while Anna swore at Dietrich in Chinese.

"Cut! Cut!" cried von Sternberg. "What is this nonsense? This is not in the script! Ladies, ladies, please stop."

Ignoring the director's pleas, the women wrestled about on the floor. Marlene grasped an empty whiskey bottle that had rolled onto the floor and smashed it over Anna's head, but it was a breakaway prop and caused no damage.

Finally, the crew members broke up the fight and separated the two women.

"Marlene, what the hell is this all about?" queried von Sternberg.

"No one upstages Marlene Dietrich!" screamed Dietrich in German.

Mr. von Sternberg threw his arms up in the air. "Marlene, all the world loves you. A lowly Chinese tart cannot upstage you," he responded in German. He flashed an embarrassed smile toward Anna, having forgotten that she also understood German.

von Sternberg ordered an assistant to fetch a bottle of cognac that he kept in his attaché case. "My honorable divas, do you realize how ridiculous the two of you look? You both look as if you have been hit by a tornado." He removed the cap from the cognac bottle. "Dear fräuleins, I love you both. At Paramount we are all family, but like family members, we do not always agree with one another. Marlene, Anna, you are two talented actresses. There is enough limelight for the both of you." He turned to one of his assistants. "Three glasses, Dorothy."

Marlene snatched the cognac from him. "Forget the goddamn glass," she cried, and gulped down the liquor like it was water. Dietrich noticed her image reflected on a wall mirror. "I am a sorry sight," she sighed.

Anna took the cognac from her and also took a swig directly from the bottle. She then nudged Marlene off to one side so she could determine the amount of damage to her own face.

Always the diva, Dietrich gave her own nudge in return, so she could gaze again at her own face. Anna tried to push Marlene aside once more, but the German stood her ground.

"God damn it, China girl, the mirror is big enough that we can look at our ravaged faces together," she spat.

Both women had smeared lipstick, smeared mascara, and tangled hair. Standing side by side, the two women shared the bottle of cognac.

"Girlfriend, what a fine pair we make," Dietrich said in jest.

For a moment, they both looked at each other's sorry appearance, then burst out laughing, The two women kissed and hugged each other warmly. The entire crew, as well as von Sternberg, applauded the softening friction between the two strong-willed actresses. The day's shooting was canceled. They would resume the following day.

Marlene placed her arm on Anna's shoulder. "Girlfriend, come with me to my mansion in Beverly Hills. We can lick our wounds there," she laughed.

Anna agreed, and the pair left the soundstage arm-in-arm, like old friends.

20

As expected, Dietrich's home, like the homes of the most successful movie actresses, was quite grand. After one of Dietrich's maids cleansed and disinfected Anna's wounds, Anna prepared the two of them a simple but tasty meal of pork noodle soup. The women delighted each other with anecdotes of their film careers. They danced together to lively jazz music played on a phonograph, all the while drinking strong tequila. Finally, they collapsed in a drunken stupor on the living room sofa.

Mr. von Sternberg gave the women a good scolding when they arrived several hours late for the restart of filming, all the while smiling under his reprimanding words. Being a longtime friend and colleague of Dietrich's, he knew that after she had mended her fences with a co-star, she would dedicate herself fully to whatever film project they were collaborating on.

"Goddamn bloodshot eyes it is. Good thing this flicker is being shot in black and white," mouthed Anna under her breath as the make-up artist applied heavy make-up to conceal her bruises.

And so began a love-hate relationship. Daily, from the restart of the film to its completion, the two prima donna actresses would argue, shouting at each other in German. But despite their constant bickering, von Sternberg and the film crew knew the ego-centric women had a mutual respect for one another and a binding friendship.

On one of their infrequent free days from shooting, the women decided to go out for a night of drinking and dancing.

Upon entering one of Hollywood's most prestigious

nightclubs—one frequented by celebrities and people of influence, Marlene said, "Table for two, Phillip." She was a regular patron of the establishment.

The maître d' peered at the two women with disapproving eyes. It was quite unorthodox for women to patronize a nightclub without a male escort, let alone a woman of color in the 1930s.

"Um, Miss Dietrich, is this your maid?" the maître d' snapped. "My apologies. We cannot allow domestic help to sit with the patrons."

"Philip, stop being a horse's ass. You are denying access to Miss Anna May Wong, a great actress of any color. You are not good enough to kiss her yellow ass."

An etched look of growing agitation appeared on the head waiter's face. "Miss Dietrich, your lady friend's status as an actress is of no consequence to me. In any case, we have no tables available."

Dietrich surveyed the room. "Philip, I see a good many unoccupied tables," she said, giving him a smug look.

"It's all right, Marlene. We can go to your place and have a private party," said Anna, trying to defuse the awkward situation.

"No, it is not all right. In Germany, there were nightclubs that turned away my Jewish friends. Being a polite fool, I did not speak up. But tonight I will not tolerate such hateful bigotry!" exclaimed Marlene as she snatched the reservation list from the head waiter's hand and began tearing it to shreds.

Bits of paper rained down as the head waiter stood there, quite stunned. "Uh, very well, Miss Dietrich, I will make an exception," he spoke, trying to avoid negative publicity for the nightclub.

"Fräulein Marlene, you have the balls of a Manchu," quipped Anna as another waiter seated them.

Marlene kissed Anna on the mouth. "Girlfriend, when the camera rolls I will always be your rival, but once the camera stops we will be good friends forever."

They ordered a bottle of Dom Pérignon in celebration of their friendship. Many of the other patrons stared at the odd couple.

As predicted by the studio head and von Sternberg, *Shanghai Express* was a huge success. Much to Dietrich's chagrin, the critics wrote glowing praise of Anna's powerful, intense performance as a reformed prostitute. But despite Dietrich's unwillingness to share the glory, she nonetheless liked Anna. Like herself, Anna was a spirited, independent woman in a male-controlled world.

But gradually, as with many friendships, time and circumstance caused Anna and Marlene to drift apart. An actor's life is one of a vagabond. Both women left Hollywood for extended periods to act in movies and in Broadway plays. Anna would find out that Marlene began a torrid affair with her childhood friend, John Wayne. Never being romantically involved with Wayne, she was pleased that her two friends were in a relationship.

As a result of her success with *Shanghai Express,* the movie offers were now pouring in for Anna. With her renewed success, she fulfilled a second lifelong dream by visiting the land of her ancestors. To her disappointment, the citizens of China, and even her relatives she had never met before, gave Anna a cold reception. China in the 1930s was still traditionally conservative and unaccustomed to an emancipated, straight-talking woman. It mattered little to them that on the Gold Mountain, Anna May Wong was a famous movie actress.

But even if she had been treated more warmly, Anna was forced to cut her visit short due to growing unrest in the country. Like the aggressive Nazis in Europe, the Japanese war mongers were intent on conquering China and, undoubtedly, the whole of Asia and the Pacific Island nations. As Anna boarded a steamer in Hong Kong bound for the United States, she learned from the newspapers of the Japanese armed forces capturing Nanking, the provisional capital of China, and the horrific atrocities the Japanese soldiers were carrying out on the capital's citizenry. Despite the chilled welcome she received in China, Anna rallied her fellow Chinese residing in America to form a relief fund to aid the beleaguered citizens of

China.

Now in her early thirties, Anna had committed herself to appearing only in films with positive portrayals of Chinese characters. In 1937, Anna acted in one of her finest roles, *Daughter of Shanghai.* It was one of the rare Hollywood films of any era that was Asian-themed with actual Asian actors in the lead roles. Anna played the role of Lan Ying Lin, who sought her father's murderer.

Shortly after the success of *Daughter of Shanghai,* Anna's agent rushed into her home unannounced.

"Ben, have you ever heard of the Chinese custom of knocking before entering?" teased Anna.

"My apologies, Anna, but I have the most wonderful, exciting news!" exclaimed her agent as he dropped a book in her lap.

"The Good Earth, written by Pearl S. Buck," spoke Anna, reading the title and author's name out loud. "What is this book to me?" she added.

Ben hugged Anna with excited giddiness. "Anna, my sweet client and friend, it's your ticket to super-stardom and possibly an Oscar with your name on it. Pearl Buck is a writer who specializes in writing Chinese-themed novels. *The Good Earth* is a corker. She won the Nobel Prize for this novel. It's an awesome story about a poor Chinese farmer and his family who lose everything to those pesky locusts. It's a real tear-jerker. The female lead, O Lan, who is the farmer's wife, is a role tailor-made for you. At the very least, you should get the supporting role of the concubine if you lose out to the female lead. MGM has purchased the book. I have already arranged for your audition with them, for both the female lead and the concubine role. Hopefully, you'll get the lead role. Anna, you are already a star but with *The Good Earth*, you will be a goddamned supernova!"

Anna stared at the book as if mesmerized by the title. "Yes, I've heard of Buck. She lived with her missionary parents in China for many years. O Lan is the role of a lifetime. When is my audition?"

Her voice quivered. She knew this role would change her life.

"Next week on Tuesday, at nine a.m. sharp, MGM Studios, Stage 8. And come with steel balls. A lot of white bitches have already told L.B. Mayer they want to play O Lan."

Anna hurled the novel at the wall. "Bullshit! O Lan is Chinese. I am Chinese! That role belongs to me! Why would MGM even consider giving the role to a gwah lo bitch?"

"Because they can," responded her agent with cold reality. Ben placed a reassuring hand on Anna's shoulder. "My ace client, I expect a handsome commission when you get the O Lan role. I am so proud and honored to have you as a client. Good luck, Anna." Ben kissed her on the forehead, then left.

Anna peered out the window and watched her agent drive away. She then gingerly lifted the novel off the floor. She felt ashamed for treating the book so disrespectfully. Though she had never read Pearl S. Buck's books, she had heard that the writer portrayed the Chinese characters in her books with dignity, unlike Hollywood films, which often portrayed the Chinese as stereotyped clichés.

She sat down, turned on a reading lamp, and began reading the acclaimed novel from beginning to end, without a break, all the while carefully studying the lead female character O Lan. On a notepad, she jotted down anything that referred to O Lan: her words, her appearance, her interaction with her husband, her children, her husband's mistress, and so on. After she finished reading the novel, Anna walked back and forth in front of a full-length mirror, experimenting with various gaits in the manner in which a peasant might walk, while speaking dialogue from the book in different voice reflections.

Never having had children, she had to dig deep within her soul to convey how a protective mother would think and act when her children were faced with starvation after losing everything she and her husband had worked hard for.

She visited her parents to deliver the good news about the possibility of her significant and enriching role, which would greatly honor the Chinese culture. She also asked to borrow her grandmother's peasant clothes, which had been stored in a dusty steamer trunk for many years. Overjoyed, her parents spoke of a lavish party to celebrate the momentous occasion.

To Anna's delight, the laundry employees erupted in raucous applause when Lee You announced to them in Chinese her daughter's epic role. This time, Sam Sing did not protest his employees taking a moment from work to praise the daughter he was truly proud of.

"I could not be more proud of you than if you were a man," proclaimed Sam Sing to his daughter.

Anna fought back tears, knowing this was one of the few, if not the only time, her father had praised her, although it was a questionable compliment.

On the day of her scheduled audition, Anna rose early to rehearse for the thousandth time. When she felt she was as ready as she would ever be, Anna poured herself a full glass of expensive whiskey, which she had been saving for just such an occasion. She held the glass high, admiring the golden-amber liquid. Anna reflected on her first acting role at age fourteen, when she had been one of five hundred extras in the 1919 film *The Red Lantern.*

"I wanted to be noticed, and I suppose I was, but gwah los and even my own people have short memories. The fame was so hard-fought for me. To play O Lan in *The Good Earth* would keep my name on the gwah los' lips a few more years. And to have my name on the Oscar, a few more years after that," voiced Anna under her breath. She placed the whiskey glass to her lips, then hesitated, smiling slyly as she poured the whiskey back into the bottle. *I need a clear head to impress the people at the audition. If there is a God of any color, please give me the role of O Lan to give my life value,* thought Anna.

She nearly jumped out of her skin when she heard the doorbell. It sounded like a death knell. She then remembered that the studio was sending a limousine to drive her to the audition.

On the short ride to MGM Studios, Anna read dozens of pages of notes, searching for anything that might give her an edge in her audition. Upon arriving at the studios, the limousine stopped at Stage 8. As Anna walked to the door, she rubbed her hand on the number eight that was painted on a sign. "A good omen. We Chinese consider eight a lucky number," spoke Anna under her breath.

Nervously, she opened the door to the soundstage. Inside sat one woman and a number of men wearing business suits. Anna immediately recognized a tall, middle-aged man with thinning hair and a narrow, pointy nose as being Louis B. Mayer, the head of MGM Studios. His squinty, bespectacled eyes made him look more like a bookkeeper than one of the most powerful men in Hollywood.

Mayer rushed forward to enthusiastically embrace her. "Anna May Wong, your reputation precedes you. I was quite impressed with your performance in *Shanghai Express*. You upstaged that prima donna Marlene Dietrich. Not exactly an easy task."

Beside Mayer stood another man with a weathered face and graying hair.

"Miss, it is my great honor to introduce you to Sydney Franklin, the director of our little film," announced Mayer, who then introduced the other men as assistants and the one woman as his personal secretary.

Both Mayer and Franklin were surprised to see Anna attending the audition dressed in full character as a hard-pressed Chinese peasant woman, complete with soiled face and rough hands, which she had accomplished by rubbing them with coarse sand over the last few days.

A man entered the room. He had a very common appearance.

"Paul, so glad you could join us," voiced Mayer, shaking his hand firmly.

"Miss, it is my pleasure and honor to present to you one of Hollywood's finest actors, Paul Muni. He has the male lead in *The Good Earth* project," announced Franklin.

Anna seethed with contempt at seeing yet another gwah lo man chosen to play an Asian character, but nevertheless, she hid her true feelings. She knew she had to play the role of the obedient lackey once again to have any chance to play O Lan. She would deal with her personal feelings later.

For ten hours Anna read lines from *The Good Earth* script, often interacting with Muni, at times at the insistence of the director. Anna read her lines in Chinese even though it was an English-speaking film.

The following day, she read for the concubine role. For five more days Anna auditioned for long hours. At the end of the exhausting audition process, Muni and the director had nothing but glowing praise for her acting talents. In parting, all three men— Mayer, Franklin, and Muni—took turns embracing her. But they said nothing about her being accepted for the roles or not. Mayer only mentioned, as if in passing, that they would contact her soon regarding their decision.

For the next week, Anna could not eat or sleep. She paced back and forth in her tiny garden, chain-smoking dozens of cigarettes a day. The phone sat on a lawn table attached to a long extension cord. Whenever the phone rang, Anna almost leaped out of her skin. But each time the call was nothing of consequence.

After dark, Anna lay on the lawn chair gazing at the stars.

No one understands O Lan as I do. I have her soul, her mind, and her heart. Why are they taking so long to tell me that the role is mine? she thought. As she saw a shooting star streak across the sky, then quickly burn out, she recalled a terrible dream she'd had years ago, in which the police had beaten her savagely. She tried to grab a statue, and her fingertips were only an inch or two away from it, but some invisible force pulled her away. She was only a teenager at the time and had no inkling what the dream meant, but now as a full-grown woman, she knew it meant that the Academy Award would never be hers. But did it mean that she would be accepted for the role of O Lan? Or would she not even have the chance to play O Lan?

The doorbell rang. Fatigued from lack of sleep, Anna staggered to the door. She was startled to see Marlene Dietrich standing on the doorstep at that late hour.

Anna was thrilled. "Marlene, darling! We have not seen each other for over a year!" she said as she ushered her friend inside. "It is nearly midnight. To what do I owe the honor of this visit at such a late hour?" Anna gazed at her watch.

The normally jovial woman seemed troubled by something. "Anna, darling, do you have a touch of cognac or whiskey for an old friend?"

Anna invited Marlene to sit as she fetched the whiskey. She poured a small measure into a glass. Marlene grabbed the bottle and continued to pour whiskey until the glass was nearly full. She then gulped down the liquor.

"Girlfriend, you need a stiff drink before you tell me why you're here?"

Marlene nodded. "Anna, my beloved sister, MGM has chosen another actress for the female lead in *The Good Earth.*"

Anna sat down in complete shock. "And what gwah lo bitch did they choose to play O Lan?" asked Anna, knowing they had undoubtedly picked a Caucasian actress.

"Luise Rainer. I am so sorry. I know how much that role meant to you."

Anna wanted to cry but her strong pride prevented her from doing so. "Those bastards at MGM waited till this late hour to make a decision?" commented Anna.

Marlene pulled her chair beside Anna's and wrapped her arm around her.

"Sidney Franklin and L.B. Mayer made the decision yesterday. Mayer's secretary was going to call you to inform you of their decision. I told them I would deliver the sad news to you. It took this long to work up enough nerve to come here."

Anna took a swallow of whiskey directly from the bottle. "Those sons-of-bitches never wanted me to begin with," she muttered. "They were only going through the motions of auditioning me to ease their own consciences. My guess is they had already chosen Rainer before they even auditioned me."

Marlene chuckled as she took the bottle from Anna's hand and also drank directly from it. "Actually, they considered a number of white actresses for the role of O Lan, including this bitch, but chose Rainer because Franklin said she has a nice, exotic look about her."

"Certainly more exotic than this face," quipped Anna, pointing at her face. "And what of the role of the concubine?"

"That role goes to Tillie Losch."

Anna giggled painfully. "The concubine only has a couple of scenes in the flicker. They don't even think I am good enough to play a whore!"

Marlene kissed her on the cheek. "Think of all the good roles you have played, and will play, in future movies. You have touched a lot of lives, especially those of little Chinese girls who, for the first time, have realized that their lives have value. There will be other O Lan roles available to you someday."

Overcome with emotion, Anna dropped to her knees and pounded the floor with her fists. "Bullshit! I appeared in my first movie in 1919, and here it is, nearly twenty years later, and the gwah lo directors and studios still think Asian actors are not worthy of playing Asian characters in Hollywood films!"

Marlene knelt down beside Anna, holding her like a wounded child.

"Marlene, is God a white man?" queried Anna in a shaky voice.

Marlene shook her head with a sigh. "Sister, I suppose it does appear that way, but remember this: you did upstage me in *Shanghai Express*. And *no one* upstages Marlene Dietrich! You can take some satisfaction from that."

Anna pushed Marlene away and stood up. Marlene then rose to her feet and smoothed out Anna's mussed hair. She placed her hands on Anna's shoulders.

"Sister, even gwah lo movie stars do not always get what they want. Did you know that I was in love with your childhood friend,

John Wayne? I loved him and I thought he loved me, but he married another woman, perhaps under studio pressure. I do not know. Girlfriend, stop feeling sorry for yourself and get back to work. Someday, another *Good Earth* will come along with another character like O Lan, and when that day comes, I will fight with you for that role. In the meantime, I will spend the night with you and we'll get drunk together. I will send my chauffeur to the market to purchase some good veal and I will cook you a fine dinner of schnitzel."

"Leave, Fräulein Dietrich," spoke Anna sharply.

Marlene reached out to touch Anna, only to have her turn away.

"Leave!" snapped Anna with deep despondence, knowing that there was nothing Dietrich could say or do to lift her spirits.

"It's an unfair world we live in. Please, if you need someone to talk to, call me," voiced Marlene as she jotted down her number on a piece of paper.

Anna did not bother to look at Dietrich as she exited. Her eyes stared at the floor.

She sat on the floor drinking whiskey, cognac, and whatever else she could find in her liquor cabinet. Around noon the next day, she awoke quite hungover. Anna knew she would have to deliver the bad news to her parents. She had been confident to the point of arrogance that MGM would choose her for the role of O Lan, and now she had the humiliating task of telling her parents otherwise. She had a splitting headache. As she attempted to make a pot of coffee with trembling hands, she spilled coffee grounds on the floor. She slammed the coffee pot against the wall in frustration. With no more liquor left in the liquor cabinet, she rummaged through the kitchen cabinets. She found a bottle of cooking sherry and greedily drank the half-full bottle until it was empty.

Anna was a horrific site. Streaks of black mascara ran down her cheeks. Her dress was badly wrinkled. In a slurred voice, she phoned a taxi service to drive her to Chinatown. On the way there, her mind was in a fog after her all-night drinking binge. Anna knew that only in a drunken state could she work up the nerve to inform her parents that she would not play the role of O Lan in *The Good Earth*. Anna's mind was so blurred she hadn't bothered to put on shoes before leaving the house. As the taxi stopped in front of her parents' laundry, Anna, looking bedraggled, took a deep breath and walked inside barefoot.

21

Anna stood sheepishly in the doorway to the laundry. The employees quickly noticed her and began to shout words of praise.

"O Lan! O Lan!" they cheered.

Even her parents were in a festive mood and greeted her with excitement.

"Daughter, you look terrible," said Lee You. "Have you been celebrating your movie role?"

Anna shook her head and wobbled. "Father, I suppose you were right. I am nothing but a worthless nui doi. Only children with a penis have value. I did not get the O Lan role. I was not even good enough to play the concubine. You should have drowned me in the ocean like you wanted to when I was born." Anna laughed in a sad way. "Now it's too late."

Both parents gazed at their daughter, confused.

"Anna dear, you told us you already had the role. We were planning a party for you, complete with expensive bird's nest soup," stated Lee You as she pointed to the helium-filled party balloons sitting in one corner of the room.

Anna laughed. "Mother, as the gwah los say, I counted my chickens before the eggs were hatched. My pompous arrogance made me think MGM would not entertain anyone else but the talented Anna May for the O Lan role. Unfortunately, I look too 'Chinesey' for the part. They gave the role of O Lan to the round-eyed bitch Luise Rainer. Her only qualification is that she is white."

After Anna announced the bad news, the employees turned their backs to her, behaving as though she were invisible. Sam Sing slapped her face, but Anna did not feel a thing, being numb from the massive amounts of alcohol she had consumed.

"Anna, you need to take care of yourself. You look like shit. You are disgracing your mother and me and all of my workers. You need to clean yourself up," scolded Sam Sing. "Why could you not have been like other Chinese girls, and found a good husband and provided your parents with beautiful grandchildren? No, you had to be different by becoming an Asian movie star. To the gwah los, you are nothing but a sideshow freak!" He slapped her again.

"Enough!" snapped Lee You. "Leave our daughter alone. Anna is a highly respected movie actress. She is not a freak. So she lost out on an important role. We must honor her for the films she has already made and films she will do in the future."

"To hell with our daughter's acting!" screeched Sam Sing. "She's spent a career playing whores. That is what gwah los think all Chinese women are, and our precious daughter's roles only prove it." He turned his back on Anna to resume his work.

Lee You hugged Anna. "Don't listen to your father. He is a proud Chinese man. One silly movie is not the end of the world. Give your father some time to cool off. You are still our daughter, no matter what. Do not think less of yourself because of one silly movie."

Anna smiled in a sad way, then kissed her mother. "Good-bye, Mama."

"Anna, let me call you a taxi," spoke Lee You as Anna left the building.

Ignoring her mother's offer, Anna proceeded to walk the several miles back to her home across town. Soon her feet began to blister and bleed. A police patrol car pulled over to the curb beside her.

"Hey lady, do you have any identification?" queried the officer.

Anna showed no response and she continued walking.

Again the officer asked for her identification, and again Anna continued to walk without responding. The agitated policeman finally got out of his car, grabbed her arm, and spun her around.

"God damn it, chink, I am talking to you. We have laws in L.A. against vagrants. I will not ask you again. Show me your identification!" screeched the officer.

Anna was too distraught to have any of the policeman's attitude. She grinned slyly. "I am Anna May Wong, movie star. Your colleagues put me in the hospital because I had the brass to want to buy a red dress when I was just a teenager. The city police are very brave when it comes to beating a defenseless teenager," she snapped defiantly.

"Smart-ass chink. I'm arresting you for soliciting."

Anna laughed loudly. "Is that a fancy word for whoring? If that is what it is, I am guilty as charged. I have been a whore for the gwah los all my life," she quipped, and kicked the officer in the groin.

The policeman buckled over in pain. In retaliation, he struck Anna across the side of her head with his baton. Dazed, she was towed into the patrol car, then booked into the city jail. She spent the night in an unheated jail cell.

In the morning, Anna awoke to see a well-dressed man sitting beside her jail cot bandaging her injured head.

"Who the hell are you?" asked Anna in a labored voice.

"Guard! Bring Miss Wong and me some hot coffee," shouted the stranger. "Miss Wong, the name is Michael Brownfield. I am an attorney for Paramount. The studio is paying your bail. Those bastard policemen made a trumped-up charge against you for being some kind of streetwalker. What bullshit! I have already spoken to the district attorney and he is reducing your crime to a loitering misdemeanor. You will get off with a five-dollar fine with jail time already served." He smiled. "My apologies that MGM rejected you for the lead role in *The Good Earth*. It's their loss. Paramount has big plans for our star Chinese actress. Your next project will be *Dangerous to Know*. You will play the girlfriend of a gangster who ends up dumping you for a high-society dame so he can move up on the social ladder."

Anna began to giggle. "Mr. Brownfield, let me guess...the high-society dame is a gwah lo, right?"

The guard handed them their coffee through the bars of the jail cell.

The attorney laughed along with Anna. "By gwah lo, if you mean white, yes, the male lead dumps you for a gwah lo."

Anna threw the coffee cup against the bars, then buried her head. "God damn it, why must I always lose out to gwah lo bitches? I won't do it!" she shouted.

The lawyer placed a kind hand on her knee, only to have her slap it away. "Miss Wong, why must you be so pig-headed? I am not saying the Hollywood casting system is fair, but it's the only game in town. I suggest that you keep your goddamn mouth shut and do as you're told. Things will eventually change, just be patient. Think of yourself as a pioneer. You are forging a trail for Asian actors for years to come. If you do not get the man in the end, your future Chinese sisters will, all because of you."

"You son-of-a-bitch, you are only telling me what I want to hear. If a hundred or a thousand years pass, my Chinese brothers and sisters will still be cast as obedient monkeys. We will always be chink step'n fetch-its."

Brownfield took a sip of coffee and looked at her smugly. "Miss Wong, Paramount is offering you a living. If your principles tell you it's wrong, then just don't do it." Brownfield stood up and called for the guard. "Good day, Miss Wong."

After his departure, Anna sat waiting for them to complete the papers for her release. The guard took pity on her and gave Anna a cigarette, which she was dying for.

"Just don't do it," she grumbled. "The son-of-a-bitch knows if I don't do it, I will starve."

Besides posting bail, the studio paid for a taxi to take Anna home. Still barefoot when she entered her home, her first thought was to find a drink. She tore her house apart searching for liquor but there was none left. She had already consumed it all, even the cooking sherry. She did manage to find a few loose cigarettes in a desk drawer. Her hand shook as she tried to light a cigarette. She saw *The Good Earth* novel lying on the floor. As she stared at it, she forgot about the burning match she held.

"Ouch!" she cried as the match burned her fingers.

Anna sat on the floor beside the book. She tore out every page and formed a small mound of crumpled-up paper. Anna set the pages on fire and sat beside it, mesmerized by the flames. She seemed unconcerned that smoke was filling her house.

"Anna! My God!" screamed her agent Ben as he rushed in after smelling the smoke. Filling a pitcher with water from the kitchen, he quickly doused the burning pile of book pages. Ben then opened the windows and doors to clear the room. Both of them coughed harshly as Ben assisted Anna outside to the garden. He then ran back inside to fetch her a glass of water.

"Anna, dear, are you crazy? Lighting a fire on the living room floor? You could have killed yourself," he said, out of breath as he handed her the glass.

She gulped down the water, then drew a deep breath of clean air. "Ben, would anyone give a shit if I died? Be a good agent. Bring me a bottle of whiskey."

"You'd be better off with a cup of strong coffee," stated Ben as he went to the kitchen to prepare a pot.

A few minutes later, Ben gave Anna a much-needed, hot cup of coffee. Together the two of them sat side by side on lawn chairs.

"I'm so sorry you didn't get the part in *The Good Earth*," Ben said. "Those assholes that run Hollywood don't give a shit about good acting, only the mighty dollar. I fought hard for you at MGM. It would have been nice to get that ten percent commission if you could have gotten the part. But, my dear, I can get you a juicy role in another movie titled *Dangerous to Know*. You would play—"

Anna interrupted him with a laugh. "Goddamn it, that Paramount flunky already informed me about that movie when I was sitting in jail. That b-movie is not high art, like *The Good Earth*."

Ben shot up, towering over Anna like an angry father reprimanding his child. "Goddamn it, Anna, do you want to be a martyr with an empty belly? Then do it with some other agent. I have a family to feed. You want to be nailed to the cross, go ahead, but I ain't being nailed beside you. Take the freaking part! At least you'll be working. That's more than even some white actresses can say."

Anna lit a cigarette, shifting her eyes to the goldfish swimming in the small pond. "All right, Ben, I'll be the beggar to feed your family. Once a whore, always a whore."

Although *Dangerous to Know* was a light-weight movie, Anna's performance was elegant, beautiful, and sophisticated, as were most of her performances regardless of the overall film quality. Later that year, she received some consolation for losing *The Good Earth* role when Anna made the cover of *Look Magazine.* Below her photo was the caption: "The World's Most Beautiful Chinese Woman."

As predicted, *The Good Earth* was a huge success. A few months after its release, Anna, like millions of others, listened as they announced Luise Rainer the winner of the Academy Award for best actress on the night of the 1937 Academy Awards Ceremony. Anna drank a toast of Dom Pérignon. "That gold statue should have had my name on it," mouthed Anna under her breath a moment before gulping down the champagne. Then, as Rainer gave her acceptance speech on the radio, Anna grabbed a fireplace poker and proceeded to smash the radio to pieces.

The following day, she arrived on the set of her next movie quite drunk. The director understood Anna's bitter disappointment over *The Good Earth* movie, and delayed the day's shoot as he and his assistants pumped coffee into her and a female assistant held her up in a shower stall while cold water drenched her.

Finally coming to her senses, Anna apologized to the director and every member of the film crew, then proceeded to give a moving performance in the film.

22

With the onset of World War II, Anna continued to receive steady work, albeit mostly supporting roles. On occasion, the studios cast her in dignified, memorable roles in films such as *Bombs Over Burma,* a war drama where Anna played a schoolteacher who was in danger; and *The Lad From Chungking,* another war drama where she played a guerilla leader. Despite her reduced income, Anna auctioned off most of her exquisite wardrobe to aid the Chinese war relief. During the war years, she watched with pride as her childhood friend, John Wayne, became a major film star.

When the war ended in 1945, Anna was approaching middle-age. The days of her being cast as a sensual femme fatale were over, and though she continued to act in movies, she was generally cast as a maid or housekeeper.

With the lesser roles and reduced income, she was forced to move from her home in an upper-class neighborhood to a modest apartment in a blue-collar section of Los Angeles.

By the mid-twentieth century, the rapid rise of Communism—particularly in mainland China, the home of Anna's ancestors, and in Russia, which was increasing its military arsenal—created an atmosphere of fear and anxiety in America.

A senator from Wisconsin named Joseph McCarthy took advantage of America's exaggerated fear of the Communist threat to enhance his own political power by creating a rabid witch hunt, claiming without a shred of proof that Communist spies had infiltrated the United States government.

In a parallel witch hunt, right-wing conservatives in the film industry irrationally accused actors, directors, screenwriters, and others of being closet Communists trying to subvert the American way of life subliminally in films. Many talented people in entertainment lost their livelihoods after either being accused of Communist affiliations or for refusing to reveal the names of associates who were suspected of being Communists.

"What a crock of horse shit, Anna," snapped a make-up artist as he worked on her one day. "I had a dear buddy lose his acting contract with MGM because the Motion Picture Alliance labeled him a pinko-Commie. Commie, my ass! My buddy George is as much a Commie as George Washington was. And even if he were, what gives that prick John Wayne and his cronies the right to tell people how to live and think?"

"John Wayne? What is Wayne's connection to the Motion Picture Alliance?"

The make-up artist laughed. "Wayne is an ultra-conservative. He bleeds red, white, and blue. He is the president of the Alliance. Any poor soul in the movie business so much as wearing red socks or drinking vodka will be suspected of being a Commie, and you can forget about ever working in this town again."

A horrific look of shock flashed on Anna's face. "Johnny was my hero! He protected me against bullies when we were kids," she murmured.

"What did you say, Miss Wong?" queried the make-up artist.

"Nothing," Anna replied.

That evening, after the day's shooting, Anna purchased a newspaper on the way to her apartment. As usual, her first order of business after returning home from a long day of shooting was to go to the liquor cabinet and have a stiff drink to unwind. As she took the cap off a bottle of vodka, Anna chuckled, remembering what the make-up artist had warned her about. Returning the vodka bottle to the cabinet, she then retrieved a bottle of tequila.

While sitting at her kitchen table, Anna thumbed through the newspaper, searching for her favorite page — the Hedda Hopper column. The powerful entertainment gossip columnist had a following of twelve million readers, Anna being one of them. Sipping the tequila, she was amused as she read Hedda's innuendos as to what movie star was cheating on his or her spouse. Her mouth dropped when she came to a paragraph that read: "What washed-up Chinese movie actress is a closet Communist, spying for Red China?"

Anna could not believe her eyes. It was obvious the paragraph was referring to her. To avoid lawsuits, Hopper was never foolish enough to mention any names specifically when it came to negative gossip, but it was quite obvious to Anna and millions of readers that she was referring to her, given the fact that Anna was the first and only Asian woman to reach star status.

Anna stood up, shouting at Hopper's column in Chinese. She nearly jumped out of her skin when the phone interrupted her ranting. Reluctantly, she answered it. It was John Wayne's secretary, requesting that Anna come to his office at once. Anna thought it odd that she had been *told* to come to Wayne's office in the form of a command, rather than a request or invitation.

Anna knew the order for an audience with one of Hollywood's biggest stars would probably be something unpleasant.

I haven't seen the Duke in over ten years, she thought. *This must be because of the "red scare" that's infected so many American gwah lo fools.* She began to laugh.

As she rode in the taxi to Wayne's office, she recalled Orson Wells's Halloween joke in 1939, when his colleagues read a play on the radio about a Martian invasion of Earth. The idiot Americans thought it was a real news broadcast. Thousands of Americans went hysterical, frightened by the monster Martian invaders. "Only this time, the monster invaders are called Communists," murmured Anna.

Feeling anxious as she walked into Wayne's outer office, Anna repeated to herself what good childhood friends she and the Duke were. *Such a dear friend would not harm me. He would do nothing other than slap my wrist if I am here to be dressed down.*

"Miss Wong what a pleasant surprise to meet you at last," said the secretary as Anna introduced herself. "Mr. Wayne told me the two of you have been friends as far back as grade school."

"Mary! Send in my China doll!" came a booming voice from the inner office.

Anna entered the office. The tall, ruggedly handsome Wayne hugged her with such vigor that he lifted Anna off of her feet. "China doll, we've not seen each other in a coon's age. Take a chair. Sit. That's what they're made for."

Anna sat as Wayne proceeded to pour fine whiskey into two glasses, then handed one glass to Anna.

"A twenty-five-yearer. Damn good firewater. A toast to good friends!" exclaimed Wayne as he clinked glasses with her.

Together the two old friends gulped down the bourbon.

"Ah! Damn fine snake oil," voiced Wayne as a worrisome look grew on his craggy face. "Little sister, I fed yah the sugar and now the shit. It pains me to tell you that your career in Hollywood could be over. But that, my friend, is a worst-case scenario. All you need to do is give me a few names and I'll make some calls to the studios and you'll get more act'n work than there are tea bags in Chinatown," chuckled Wayne.

"Names of who, Duke?" queried Anna.

Hesitant to speak, Wayne poured a little more bourbon into her glass. "My little sister, the world grew up. It's not like my Westerns, where yah get rid of the bad guys by putting a bullet between their eyes. There is a Communist threat in this here world. A great American senator, Joseph McCarthy, is trying to root out those Commie sons-of-bitches that infiltrated the United States government. Some of my associates and I are doing the same by trying to root out those godless red bastards in the film industry."

Anna placed her glass on Wayne's desk and looked at him, disturbed by his words. "You can't be serious. You and your buddies actually believe the Communists will conquer the world by making silly movies?"

"Silly subversive movies!" shouted the Duke.

The six-foot-four-inch Wayne stood towering over her. "Goddamn it, my little sister, those Commies are not stupid enough to say 'Here, come join the Communist party.' They do it subliminally in perverse movies like *High Noon*, made by that pinko lovin' director Stanley Kramer."

Anna glared at Wayne, refusing to be intimidated by his hulking frame or star status. "Duke, my friend, are you delusional or just stupid? If my memory is correct, *High Noon* won a couple of Oscars, for best picture and for best actor, Gary Cooper. If I understand your ridiculous logic, the movie was un-American because no one in the town would lift a finger to help Cooper battle the bad guys?"

"Exactly, little sister," responded Wayne.

Anna giggled. "Duke, dear friend, where were these brave Americans when I was beaten to a pulp twenty-five years ago by the city police for refusing to leave a dress store?"

Wayne shook his head. He took two cigarettes from a pack, handed one to Anna and lit it for her, then lit his own.

"Little sister, they would have had to answer to me had I been there. Are you forgettin' how I battled your bullies when we were young'uns? Apples and oranges. Like the bastards that beat on you and your childhood bullies, there're always a few rotten apples in the basket. But most Americans, including yours truly, stand up for the little guy...or little woman." Wayne placed a blank sheet of writing paper on the desk in front of Anna. "Friend, enough banter. Make a list of your colleagues who are godless pinko Commies. Please, save America. Save yourself. In fact, I'm lookin' right now at a script called *The Conqueror*. They want me to play Genghis Khan. There's a meaty role for you as Kahn's mother. No offense, friend, we're both 'bout the same age, but the make-up artist will add some years to your face."

"Huh! John Wayne playing a Mongol. You resemble a Mongol as much as I resemble Marilyn Monroe!"

"China doll, I'm tired of playin' a cowboy hard-ass. I too want to vary my performances. But according to the casting directors, there're not enough talented Asian men to play male leads."

Anna puffed heavily on her cigarette, growing more agitated. "I've heard that bullshit before."

Wayne slammed his fists on the desk. "Enough 'bout Genghis Khan and Asian actors. Start making a list of your Commie friends, then sign it. Do you want to keep chow mein and rice in your belly, or starve? Start writing! Goddamn Chinese pride, is that it? Eddie Robinson and that Jew Elia Kazan were not too proud to name their Commie friends. I fought the Japs and Krauts in dozens of movies. Now I have to battle an enemy to America that fights dirty. Please stand with me to keep America free, my friend."

"Duke...Mr. Wayne...I am not a Communist."

Wayne grinned slyly as he pulled a newspaper from his desk drawer and dropped the paper in Anna's lap. "Not according to Hedda Hopper," spoke Wayne, pointing to Hooper's daily column.

Anna spat on the newspaper. "Miss Hopper bullshits quite colorfully to sell papers and fill her bank account, and to make herself feel significant when she could not succeed as an actress."

Wayne stood behind Anna, placing his ham-like hands on her shoulders. "Old friend, Commie or not, you know those who are, so start namin' some names and put this insanity behind us, and I'll start makin' those phone calls to the studios like I promised."

Anna stood up and began to jot down some names on the paper Wayne had laid before her. She then signed her name.

Wayne smiled with satisfaction, "Anna, I knew you were a top hand. Welcome back to the fold." He glanced at the paper, then back up at Anna. "What's this bullshit? You wrote Donald Duck and Mickey Mouse. Sister, you don't seem to understand the seriousness of the situation."

"Mr. Wayne, I do understand. You're a flag-waving diehard American patriot. Forgive me for changing the subject, but may I ask, what branch of the Armed Forces did you serve in during the

179

great World War II? Did you fight in the Pacific or in Europe—oh, excuse me...I forgot, you were shooting blanks."

Anna then proceeded to leave his office. "Duke, you were my hero at one time, but I stopped believing in heroes who use chocolate syrup in place of real blood. Good day, Mr. Wayne," she said as she walked out.

Accustomed to having his way, Wayne was at a loss for words as he watched Anna exit.

23

As Anna expected, the acting offers dried up. She managed to earn a few dollars acting at local playhouses and teaching drama classes at the Chinese children's school in Chinatown. For much of her adult life, she had been a heavy drinker, but her drinking problem was only exacerbated by no longer being able to work in the profession she loved so much. She began to neglect her health. With deep bitterness and frustration, Anna watched on the new entertainment medium called television the continued demeaning and stereotyping of Asians.

One afternoon in the mid-1950s, Anna had fallen asleep with the television on. A soft knock awakened her. "God damn it, Mrs. Watson, I'll have the rent money for you tomorrow!" Anna shouted, thinking it was the landlady pestering her for the late rent.

Slowly, the door opened and a hand holding a bouquet of red roses appeared.

"Anna, my love, you were expecting someone else?" quipped Sessue.

Anna was delighted and jumped to her feet to greet him. "Sessue! My old lover! When we last saw each other, the world war had not even begun," she said, hugging her former lover. "Please, take a chair and sit down...that's what they're made for," she added, copying one of John Wayne's favorite phrases.

Sessue was taken aback by her disheveled appearance and whiskey-soaked breath.

"Red roses. You were always a very thoughtful gentleman," spoke Anna as she sat beside him.

And so began a pleasant conversation that lasted for several hours. They especially took pleasure in reminiscing about their former glory days, the grand parties, and their adoring fans. Their memories improved with strong bourbon as the two of them drank.

"Sessue, weren't we beautiful? Weren't we beautiful?" Anna repeated several times.

Fighting back tears, Sessue kissed Anna tenderly on her lips. "You still are beautiful, my love," he whispered.

Anna gazed at her glass of bourbon, playfully swirling the drink in her hand. A deep sadness grew on her face. "Sessue, tell me something. Did I waste my life?"

Sessue began to chuckle. "No, not by a long shot. You were the world's first female Asian movie star and you still are. You gave all the people of our race their self-respect. You made our people understand that their lives have value; that when the gai jin beat you and spit on you, you get back up. A lesser man or woman would have played the white man's game to keep the paychecks coming in. But you! You are Anna May Wong, movie star! No, you did not waste your life."

Anna gazed at Sessue enigmatically. "Old friend, I was only fourteen when I appeared in my first movie. That was nearly forty years ago. After so much water under the bridge, the gwah los still stereotype Asians as houseboys, maids, or whores. I didn't exactly change the world," she lamented.

Sessue stood up to leave. "My dear, sweet Chinese lover. Perhaps in fifty or a hundred years, we will still be playing nothing but houseboys, whores, and buck-toothed evil bad guys, but thanks to you, our people will always know they are so much more." He looked at his watch. "I must go now. Good-bye, my lover. See you on the other side." Sessue kissed her warmly.

Anna would never see Sessue again, at least in person, although she delighted in watching him play the head of a POW camp in the classic *Bridge on the River Kwai* a year later.

With deteriorating health, Anna became a virtual recluse. In

1960, after many years of protest by the Chinese community, Anna, at long last, was honored with her name and footprints at Grauman's Chinese Theater. Most in attendance were middle-aged or just old; those who had lived long enough to remember when actresses were worshipped as goddesses. The applause for Anna was loud and genuine. *Hearing applause so loud that it hurts the ears is all I ever wanted,* reflected Anna.

This honor, along with an offer to play a maid in a Lana Turner film called *Portrait in Black,* invigorated the fading movie actress. Although the role was that of a stereotypical domestic servant, which Anna abhorred, it was her first opportunity to stand before a camera in over a decade.

With this small role and the revived attention from the honor of having her footprints at the renowned Grauman's Chinese Theater alongside John Wayne and Marlene Dietrich, she received a unique offer.

One evening, there was a soft knock on Anna's door, but given Anna's state of health, it sounded as loud as a church bell. "Get the hell outta here! Whatever you're selling, I already have six of them," snapped Anna in a whiskey-soaked slur.

Slowly, the door opened and a distinguished-looking, dark-haired, middle-aged man poked his head through the opening. "Um, Miss Wong, forgive me for this intrusion. I am the film producer Ross Hunter. I am producing an all-Asian musical titled *Flower Drum Song.* I wish to offer you one of the lead roles, as the matriarch of a wealthy American Chinese family. It's a very amusing love story, the two lead actors Nancy Kwan and James Shigeta have both expressed interest in working with such a screen legend as yourself. Please say yes, Miss Wong. Everyone associated with this project would be honored to work with you."

Anna, who was lying on the sofa grasping a whiskey bottle in her hand, quickly sat up and placed the bottle on the coffee table. Embarrassed by her appearance, she straightened her rumpled clothes and smoothed her tangled hair. "Mr. Hunter, have a seat. I believe I have heard of you."

Hunter took a seat and handed Anna the script to the film project. She began to thumb through the pages. "Um...interesting. Mr. Hunter, do you have a cigarette?"

"Please, call me Ross," spoke Hunter as he handed her a cigarette, then lit it for her.

Anna read the lines for the character with intensity. She then gazed at Hunter with burning eyes as if trying to read the man's mind. Inhaling the cigarette smoke deeply into her lungs, she finally spoke after a long pause. "Mr. Hunter—uh, Ross...may I ask you something? Do you really feel I am the right actress for *Flower Drum Song*, or are you just throwing an old dog a bone?"

Hunter shook his head with an amused grin. "Miss Wong, this is 1960. Nowadays, a motion picture costs into the millions to film. There is no room in this business for pity. If I didn't think you were a good fit for this role I am offering you, I would not offer it to you."

Tears began to stream down Anna's face. "Ross, I humbly accept your kind offer. I promise to give you one-hundred-ten-percent effort. I won't let you down!" exclaimed Anna.

"Excellent! I will leave this script for you to study. Next Monday I will send a limousine for you for wardrobe fittings. And by the way, here is a check for a thousand dollars as an advance. I brought it along hoping you would accept the part."

In parting, Anna embraced Hunter, holding him tightly, almost afraid to let go. "Dear man, thank you for throwing a has-been a bone, even if you did not mean to."

Hunter kissed Anna on the cheek before leaving. "Welcome back to where you belong, Miss Wong."

Holding the check in her hand, Anna danced about the room like a giddy schoolgirl. She lifted the bottle of whiskey from the coffee table and brought it up to her lips, then paused. "No, I must keep my mind clear for the role. I have not sung in a picture in twenty years."

The euphoria Anna felt was indescribable. "*Flower Drum Song* is my comeback movie," whispered Anna to herself.

With the advance in pay, she purchased a film projector so she could view her favorite films, which the studio had presented to her years before. Late one night she watched *Toll of the Sea.* She had been drinking again, even though she had sworn off alcohol. "Wasn't I beautiful? Wasn't I beautiful..." repeated Anna over and over.

As the film came to its conclusion, she felt a sharp pain in her chest. She fell off the sofa, her life snatched from her before her head hit the floor.

Anna May Wong died a couple of weeks before *Flower Drum Song* began filming. The date of her death was February 3, 1961. Anna was fifty-six years old. Doctors listed the cause of her death as a heart attack due in no small part to her chronic alcoholism.

At her funeral, Sessue Hayakawa slipped an envelope into Anna's coffin before it was lowered into the ground. It was addressed to "Anna May Wong, actress." Its contents read simply:

No, Anna, you did not waste your life.

~ The End ~

About the Author

William Wong Foey holds multiple degrees in Fine Art and Social Studies. He is an alumnus of Chico State University at Chico, CA.

William is an accomplished artist, having won dozens of awards, and is represented by galleries in Sacramento and San Francisco, CA.

For a new challenge, he took up creative writing in his mid-forties. He won an award for the first short story he ever wrote in the *Chico News & Review, 1993.*

Currently, William is working on new stories and artwork, painting and writing every day.

Mr. Foey is of Chinese-American descent and his family has resided in Red Bluff, California, since the 1850s. He is a frequent speaker about the history of the Chinese on the Gold Mountain—the Chinese term for California—including interviews on TV and in periodicals.

Mr. Foey has had a lifelong commitment to civil rights causes for women and minorities.

To contact the author, email him at: SAC7000@gmail.com